THE SMURFS AND THE EGG

TAPP
Well, turn me into a sausage if I don't...
TAPP
But... but what happened to me?

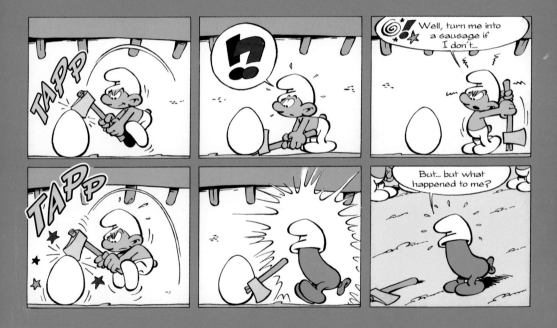

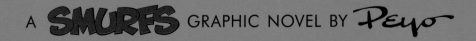

A SMURFS GRAPHIC NOVEL BY PEYO

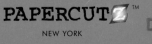

PAPERCUTZ™
NEW YORK

SMURFS GRAPHIC NOVELS AVAILABLE FROM PAPERCUTZ ™

1. **THE PURPLE SMURFS**
2. **THE SMURFS AND THE MAGIC FLUTE**
3. **THE SMURF KING**
4. **THE SMURFETTE**
5. **THE SMURFS AND THE EGG**

COMING SOON:

6. **THE SMURFS AND THE HOWLIBIRD**
7. **THE ASTROSMURF**

The Smurfs graphic novels are available in paperback for $5.99 each and in hardcover for $10.99 each at booksellers everywhere.

Or order through us. Please add $4.00 for postage and handling for the first book, add $1.00 for each additional book. Please make check payable to NBM Publishing. Send to: PAPERCUTZ, 1200 County Rd. Rte. 523, Flemington, NJ, 08822 (1-800-886-1223).

WWW.PAPERCUTZ.COM

THE SMURFS AND THE EGG

SMURF™ ©Peyo - 2011 - Licensed through Lafig Belgium -
English translation Copyright © 2011 by Papercutz.
All rights reserved.

"The Smurfs and the Egg"
BY YVAN DELPORTE AND PEYO

"The Fake Smurf"
BY YVAN DELPORTE AND PEYO

"The Hundredth Smurf"
BY YVAN DELPORTE AND PEYO

Joe Johnson, *SMURFLATIONS*
Adam Grano, *SMURFIC DESIGN*
Janice Chiang, *LETTERING SMURFETTE*
Matt. Murray, *SMURF CONSULTANT*
Michael Petranek, *ASSOCIATE SMURF*
Jim Salicrup, *SMURF-IN-CHIEF*

PAPERBACK EDITION ISBN: 978-1-59707-246-5
HARDCOVER EDITION ISBN: 978-1-59707-247-2

PRINTED IN CHINA JANUARY 2011 BY WKT CO. LTD.
3/F PHASE I LEADER INDUSTRIAL CENTRE
188 TEXACO ROAD, TSEUN WAN, N.T., HONG KONG

DISTRIBUTED BY MACMILLAN
FIRST PAPERCUTZ PRINTING

THE SMURFS AND THE EGG

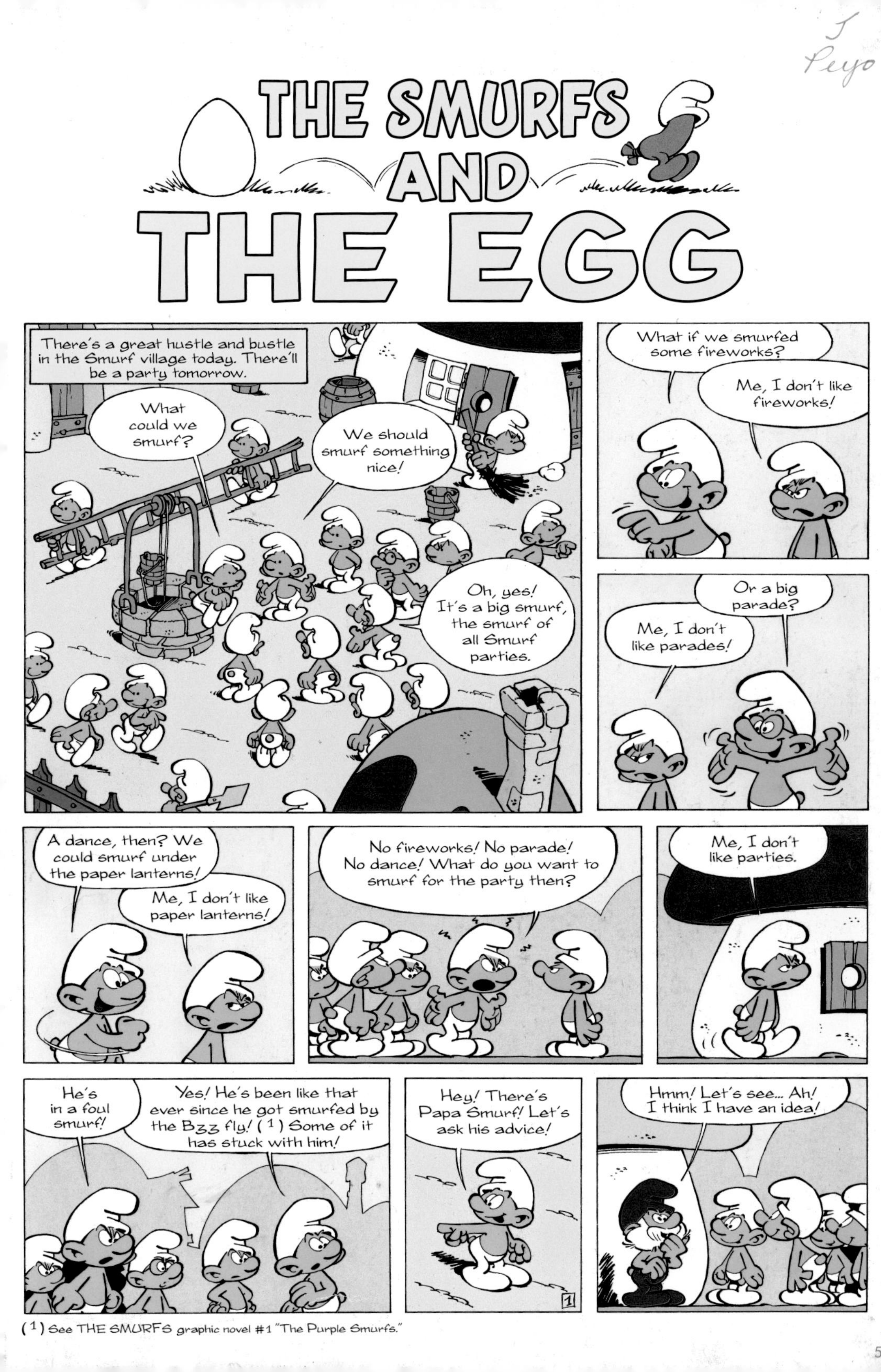
There's a great hustle and bustle in the Smurf village today. There'll be a party tomorrow.
What could we smurf?
We should smurf something nice!
Oh, yes! It's a big smurf, the smurf of all Smurf parties.
What if we smurfed some fireworks?
Me, I don't like fireworks!
Or a big parade?
Me, I don't like parades!
A dance, then? We could smurf under the paper lanterns!
Me, I don't like paper lanterns!
No fireworks! No parade! No dance! What do you want to smurf for the party then?
Me, I don't like parties.
He's in a foul smurf!
Yes! He's been like that ever since he got smurfed by the Bzz fly! (1) Some of it has stuck with him!
Hey! There's Papa Smurf! Let's ask his advice!
1
Hmm! Let's see... Ah! I think I have an idea!

(1) See THE SMURFS graphic novel #1 "The Purple Smurfs."

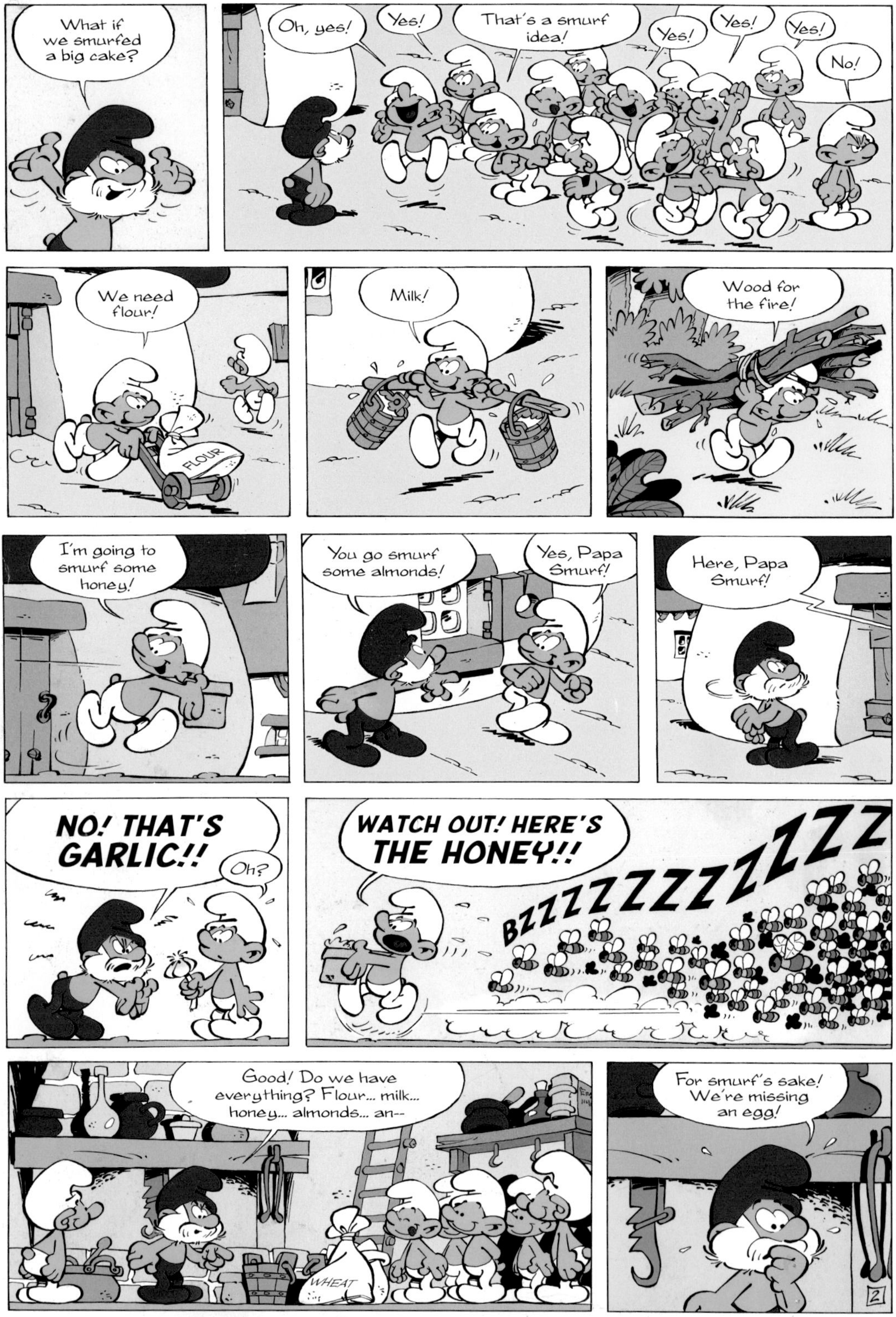
What if we smurfed a big cake?
Oh, yes!
Yes!
That's a smurf idea!
Yes!
Yes!
Yes!
No!
We need flour!
FLOUR
Milk!
Wood for the fire!
I'm going to smurf some honey!
You go smurf some almonds!
Yes, Papa Smurf!
Here, Papa Smurf!
NO! THAT'S GARLIC!!
Oh?
WATCH OUT! HERE'S THE HONEY!!
BZZZZZZZZZZZZZ
Good! Do we have everything? Flour... milk... honey... almonds... an--
WHEAT
For smurf's sake! We're missing an egg!
2

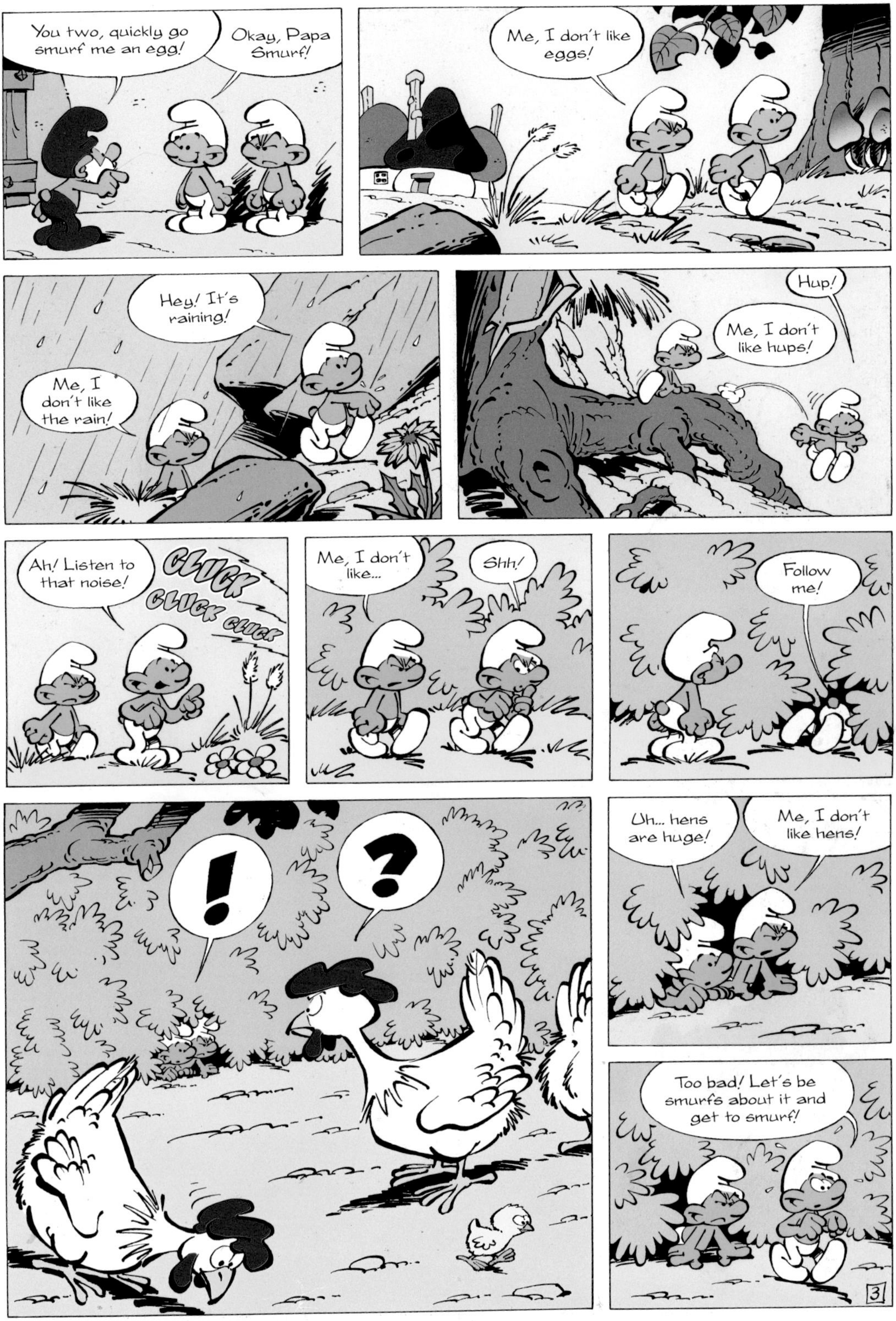
You two, quickly go smurf me an egg!
Okay, Papa Smurf!
Me, I don't like eggs!
Hey! It's raining!
Me, I don't like the rain!
Hup!
Me, I don't like hups!
Ah! Listen to that noise!
CLUCK
CLUCK CLUCK CLUCK
Me, I don't like...
Shh!
Follow me!
!
?
Uh... hens are huge!
Me, I don't like hens!
Too bad! Let's be smurfs about it and get to smurf!
3

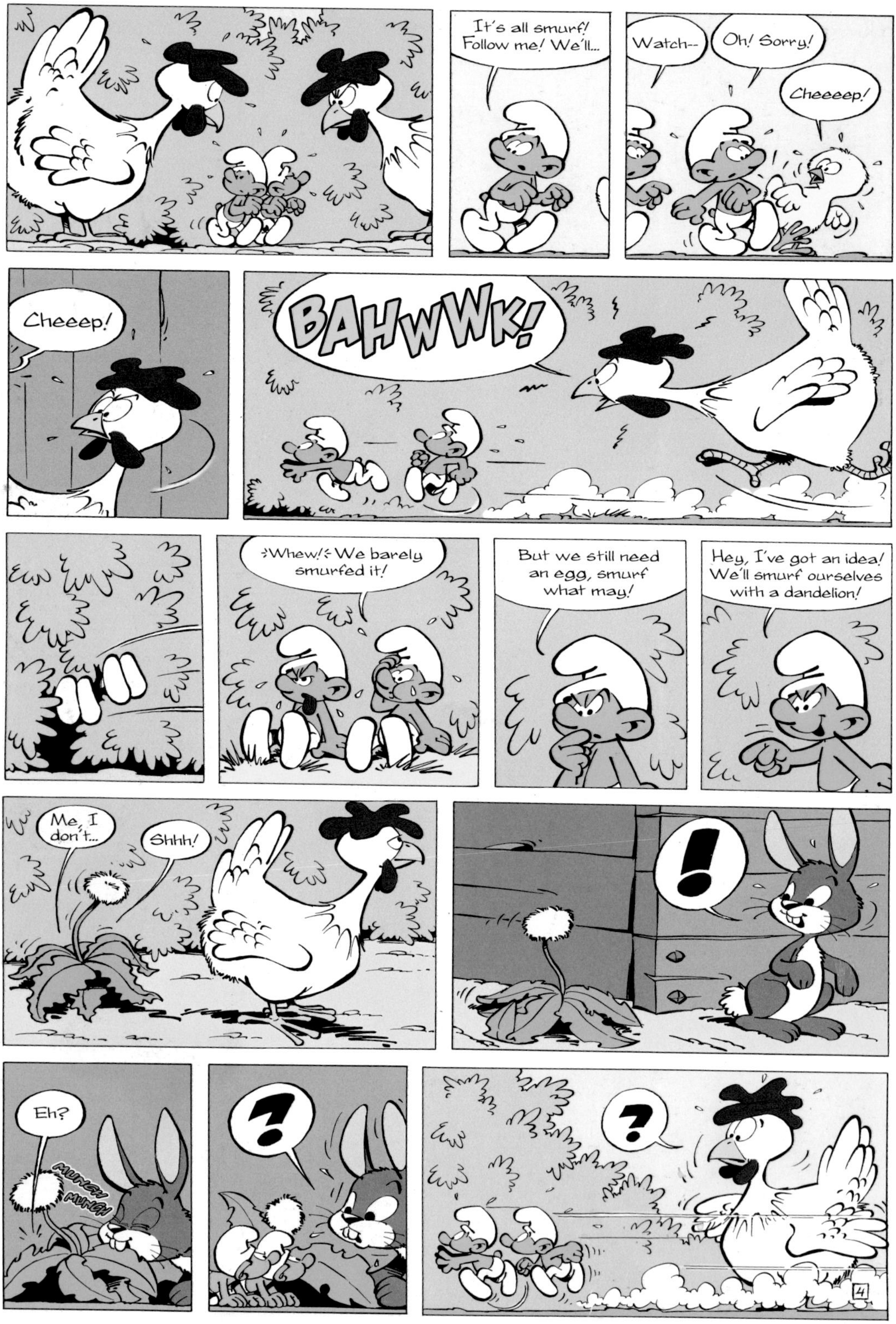

It's all smurf! Follow me! We'll...
Watch--
Oh! Sorry!
Cheeeep!
Cheeep!
BAHWWK!
Whew! We barely smurfed it!
But we still need an egg, smurf what may!
Hey, I've got an idea! We'll smurf ourselves with a dandelion!
Me, I don't...
Shhh!
!
Eh?
MUNCH
MUNCH
?
?
4

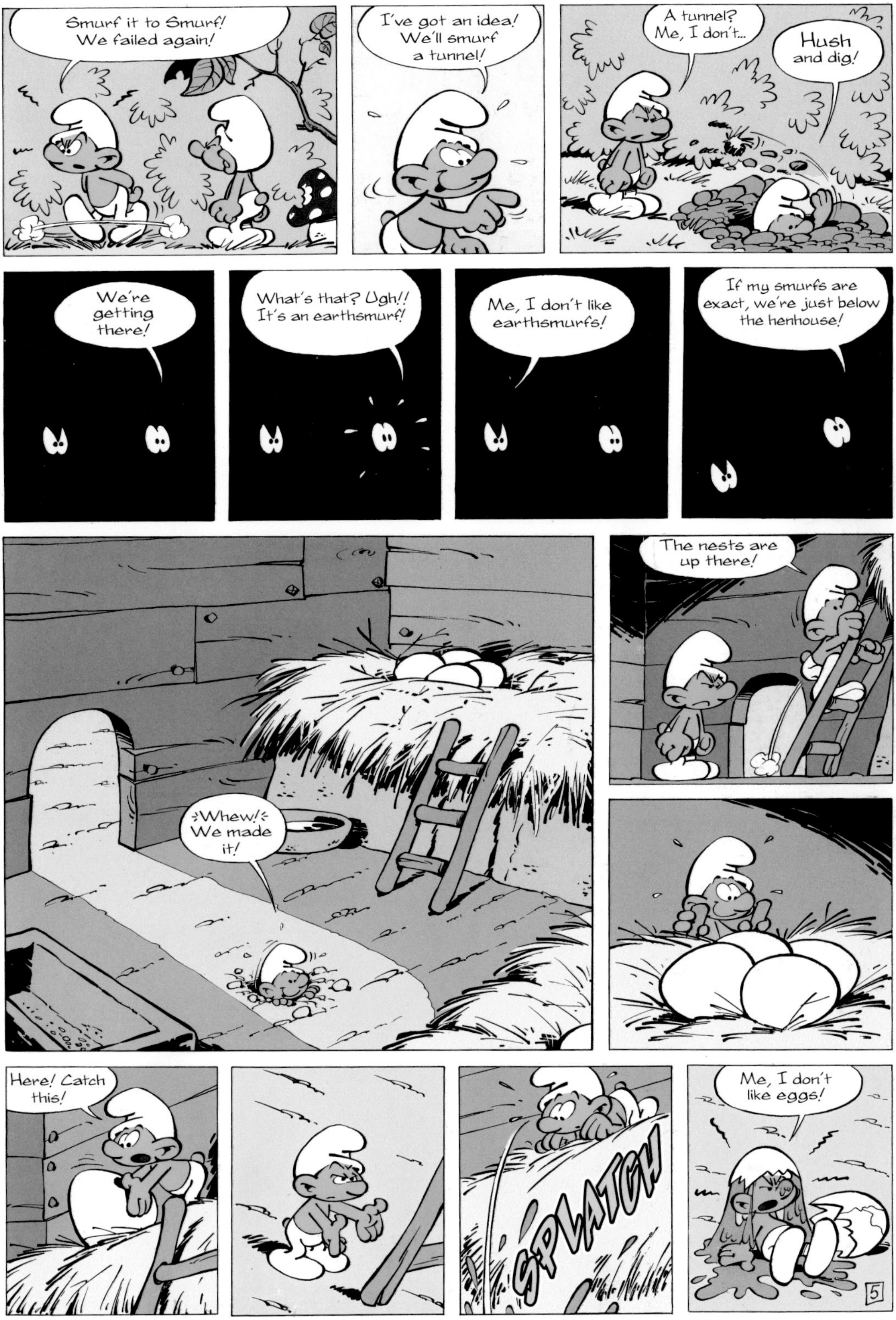

Smurf it to Smurf! We failed again!
I've got an idea! We'll smurf a tunnel!
A tunnel? Me, I don't...
Hush and dig!
We're getting there!
What's that? Ugh!! It's an earthsmurf!
Me, I don't like earthsmurfs!
If my smurfs are exact, we're just below the henhouse!
Whew! We made it!
The nests are up there!
Here! Catch this!
SPLATCH
Me, I don't like eggs!
5

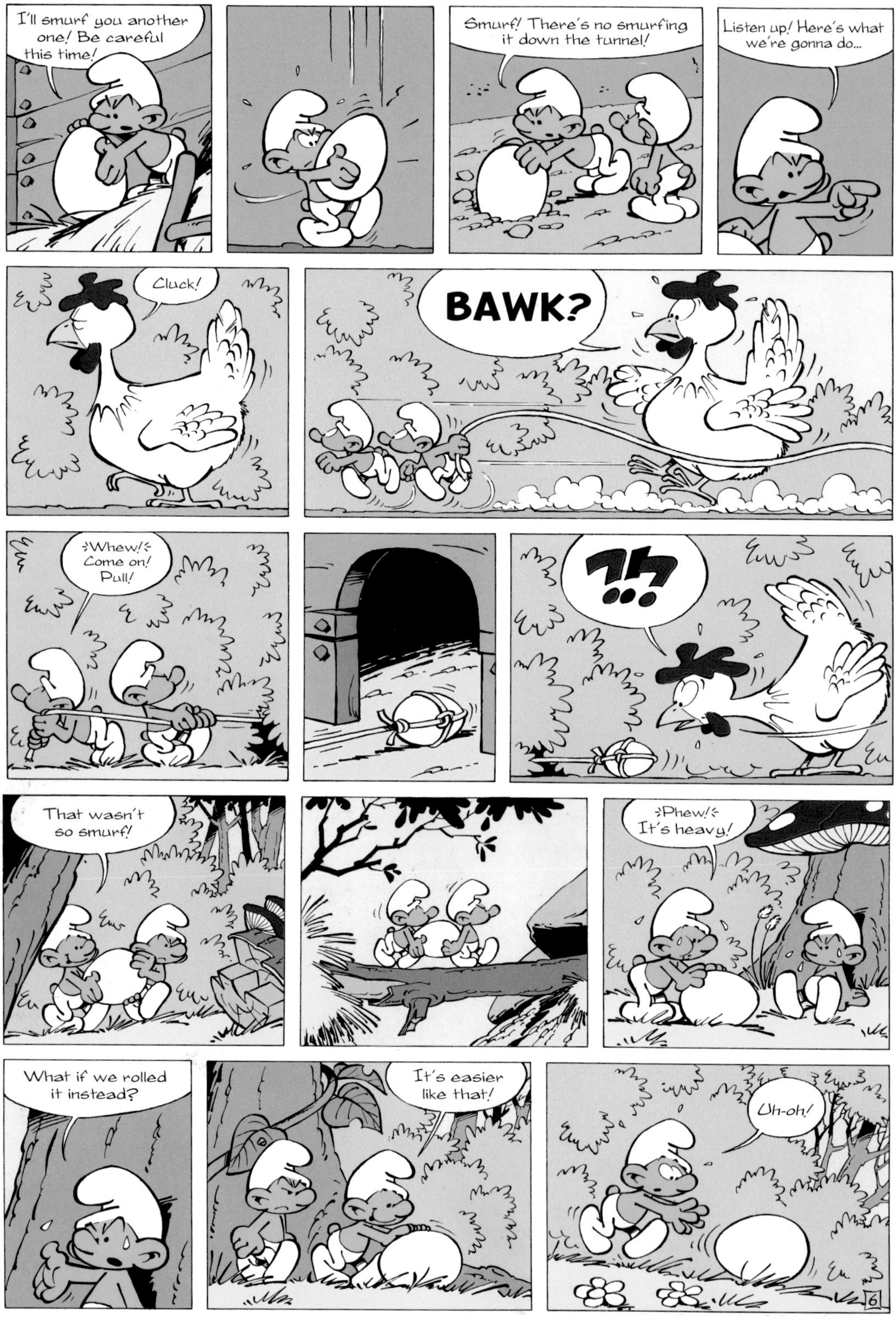
I'll smurf you another one! Be careful this time!
Smurf! There's no smurfing it down the tunnel!
Listen up! Here's what we're gonna do...
Cluck!
BAWK?
Whew! Come on! Pull!
?!...
That wasn't so smurf!
Phew! It's heavy!
What if we rolled it instead?
It's easier like that!
Uh-oh!
6

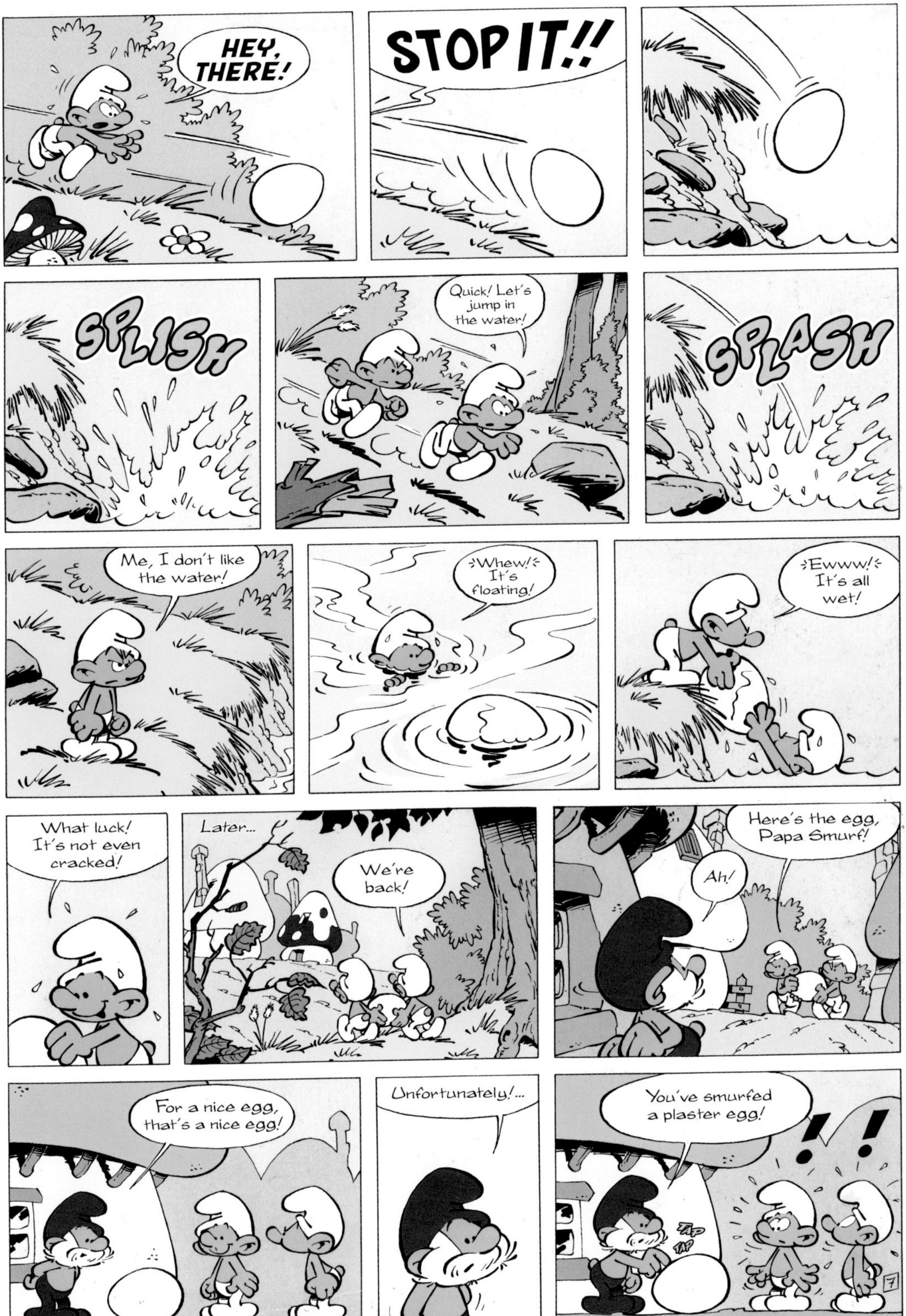
HEY, THERE!
STOP IT!!
SPLISH
Quick! Let's jump in the water!
SPLASH
Me, I don't like the water!
Whew! It's floating!
Ewww! It's all wet!
What luck! It's not even cracked!
Later...
We're back!
Here's the egg, Papa Smurf!
Ah!
For a nice egg, that's a nice egg!
Unfortunately!...
You've smurfed a plaster egg!
TAP
TAP
!!

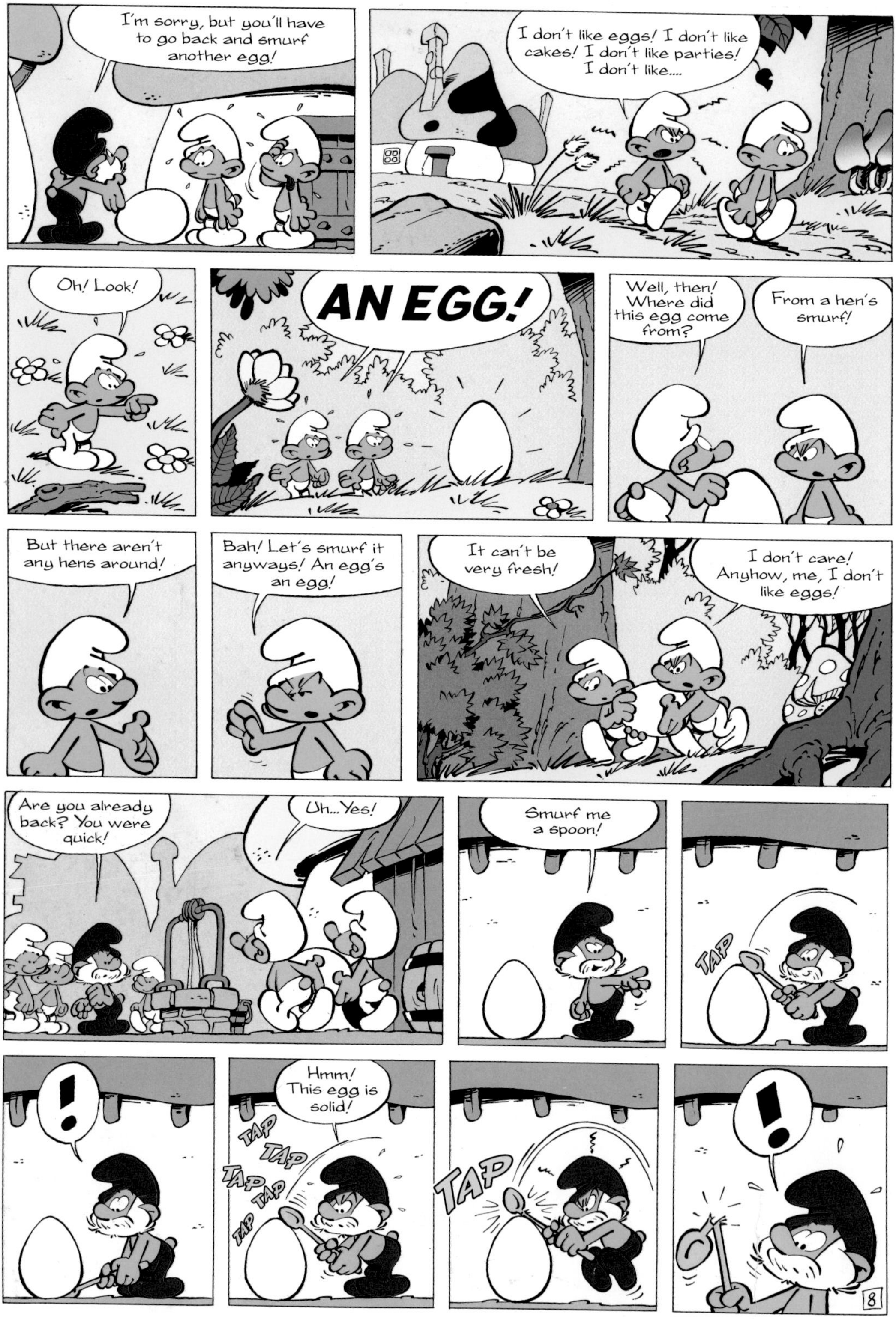
I'm sorry, but you'll have to go back and smurf another egg!
I don't like eggs! I don't like cakes! I don't like parties! I don't like....
Oh! Look!
AN EGG!
Well, then! Where did this egg come from?
From a hen's smurf!
But there aren't any hens around!
Bah! Let's smurf it anyways! An egg's an egg!
It can't be very fresh!
I don't care! Anyhow, me, I don't like eggs!
Are you already back? You were quick!
Uh... Yes!
Smurf me a spoon!
TAP
!
Hmm! This egg is solid!
TAP TAP TAP TAP TAP
TAP
!
8

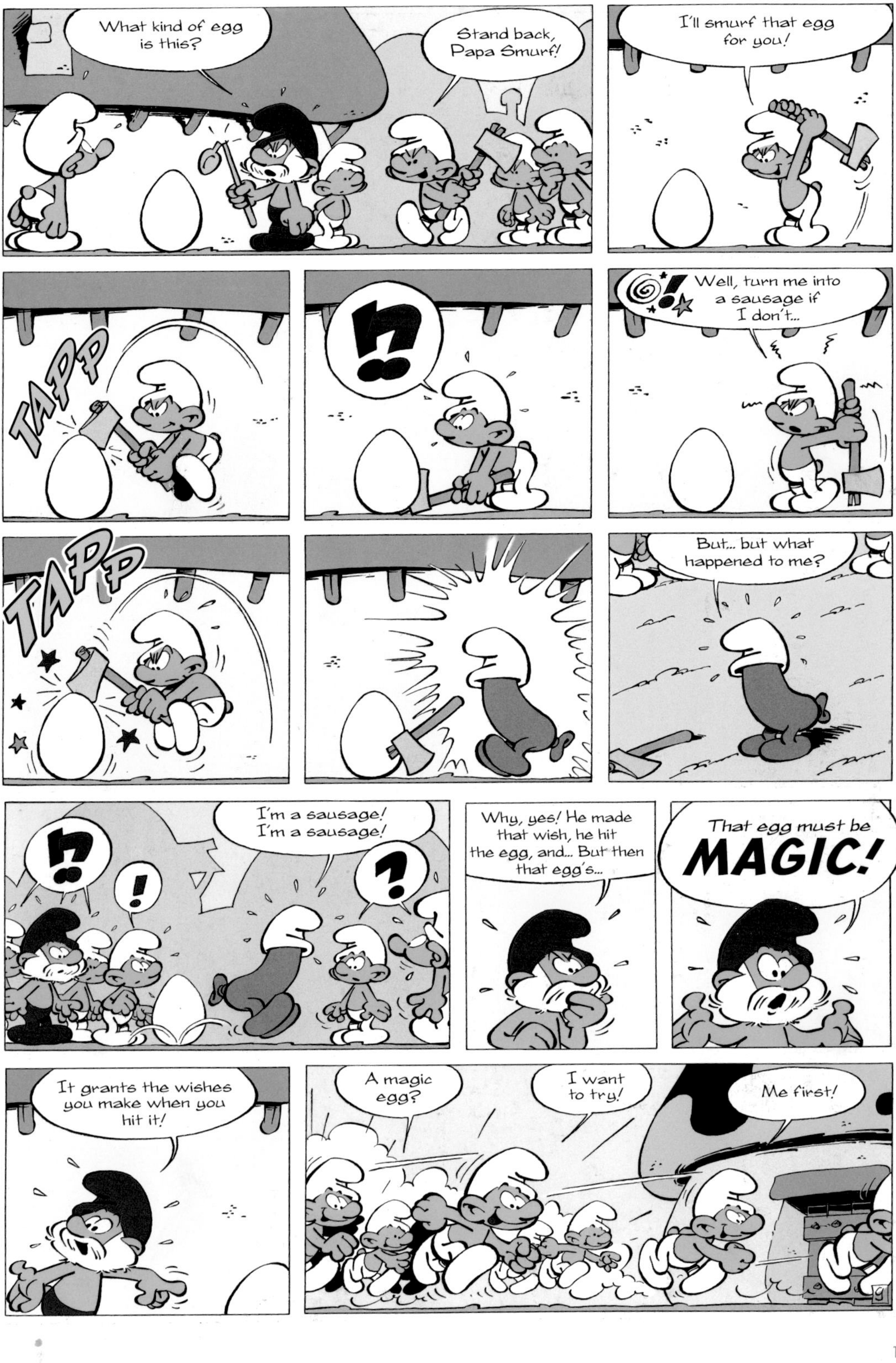

What kind of egg is this?
Stand back, Papa Smurf!
I'll smurf that egg for you!
TAPP
!?
Well, turn me into a sausage if I don't...
TAPP
But... but what happened to me?
!?
!
I'm a sausage! I'm a sausage!
?
Why, yes! He made that wish, he hit the egg, and... But then that egg's...
That egg must be MAGIC!
It grants the wishes you make when you hit it!
A magic egg?
I want to try!
Me first!

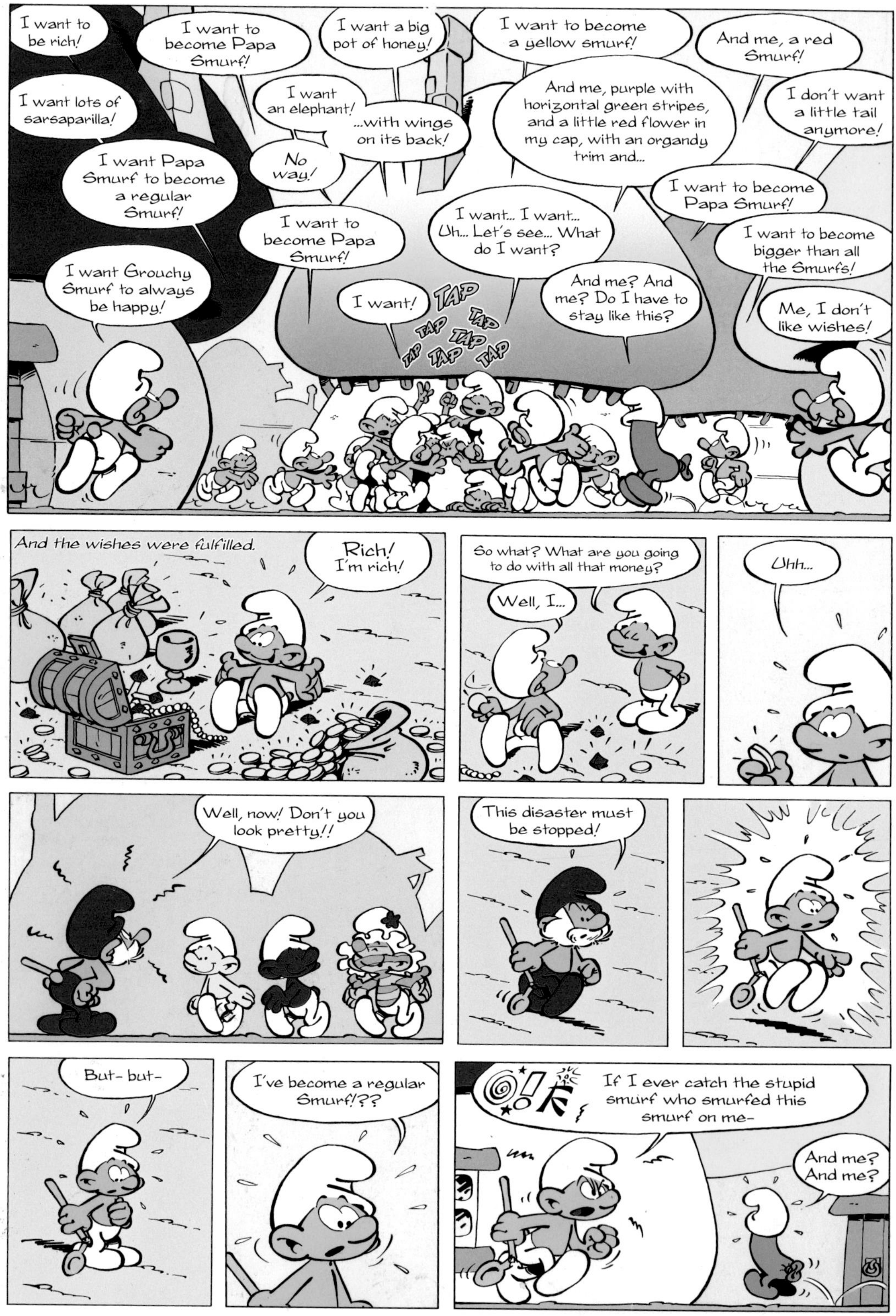
I want to be rich!
I want to become Papa Smurf!
I want a big pot of honey!
I want to become a yellow smurf!
And me, a red Smurf!
I want lots of sarsaparilla!
I want an elephant!
...with wings on its back!
No way!
And me, purple with horizontal green stripes, and a little red flower in my cap, with an organdy trim and...
I don't want a little tail anymore!
I want Papa Smurf to become a regular Smurf!
I want to become Papa Smurf!
I want... I want... Uh... Let's see... What do I want?
I want to become Papa Smurf!
I want to become bigger than all the Smurfs!
I want Grouchy Smurf to always be happy!
I want!
TAP TAP TAP TAP TAP TAP TAP
And me? And me? Do I have to stay like this?
Me, I don't like wishes!
And the wishes were fulfilled.
Rich! I'm rich!
So what? What are you going to do with all that money?
Well, I...
Uhh...
Well, now! Don't you look pretty!!
This disaster must be stopped!
But- but-
I've become a regular Smurf!??
If I ever catch the stupid smurf who smurfed this smurf on me-
And me? And me?

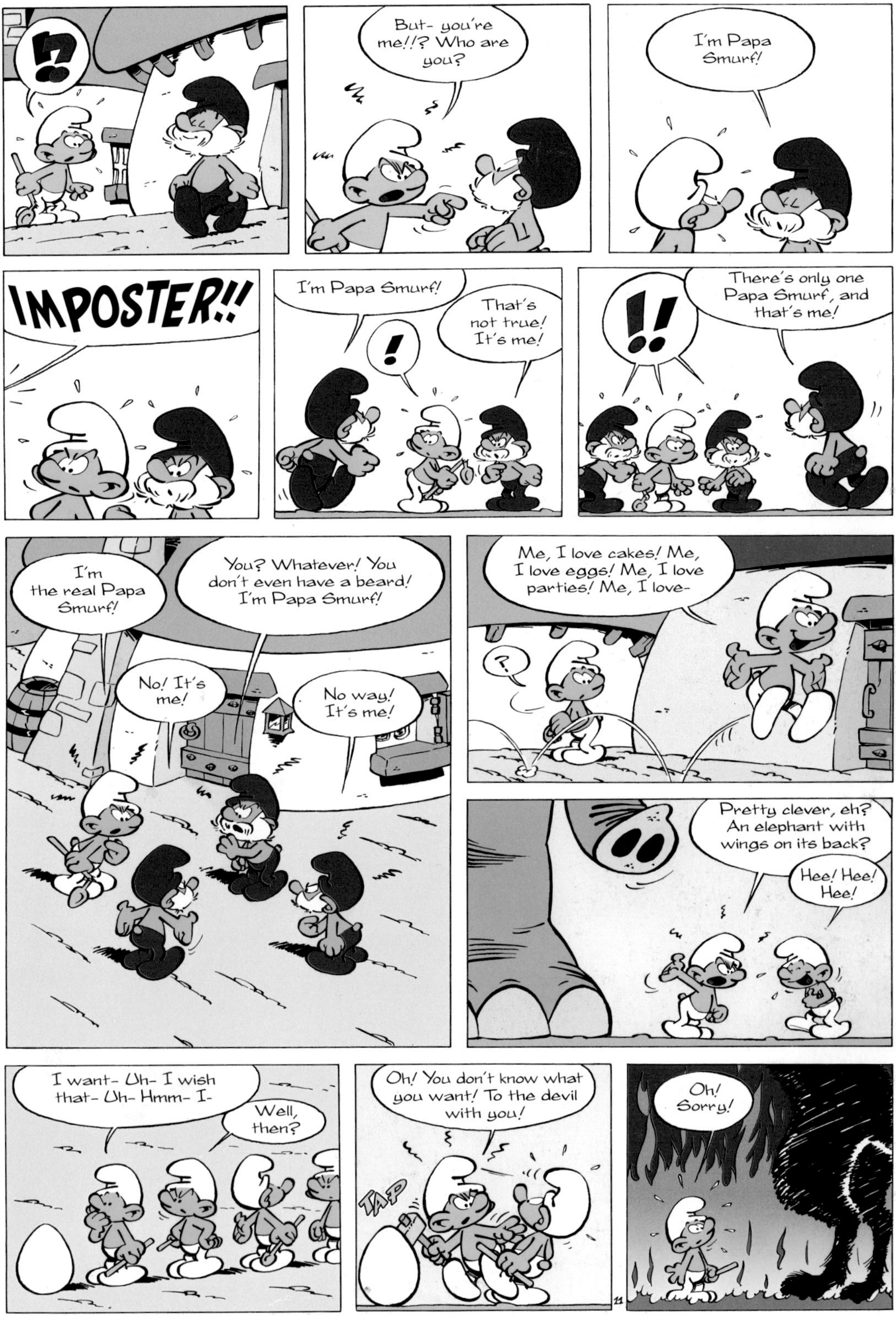

!?
But- you're me!!? Who are you?
I'm Papa Smurf!
IMPOSTER!!
I'm Papa Smurf!
!
That's not true! It's me!
!!
There's only one Papa Smurf, and that's me!
I'm the real Papa Smurf!
You? Whatever! You don't even have a beard! I'm Papa Smurf!
No! It's me!
No way! It's me!
Me, I love cakes! Me, I love eggs! Me, I love parties! Me, I love-
?
Pretty clever, eh? An elephant with wings on its back?
Hee! Hee! Hee!
I want- Uh- I wish that- Uh- Hmm- I-
Well, then?
Oh! You don't know what you want! To the devil with you!
TAP
Oh! Sorry!

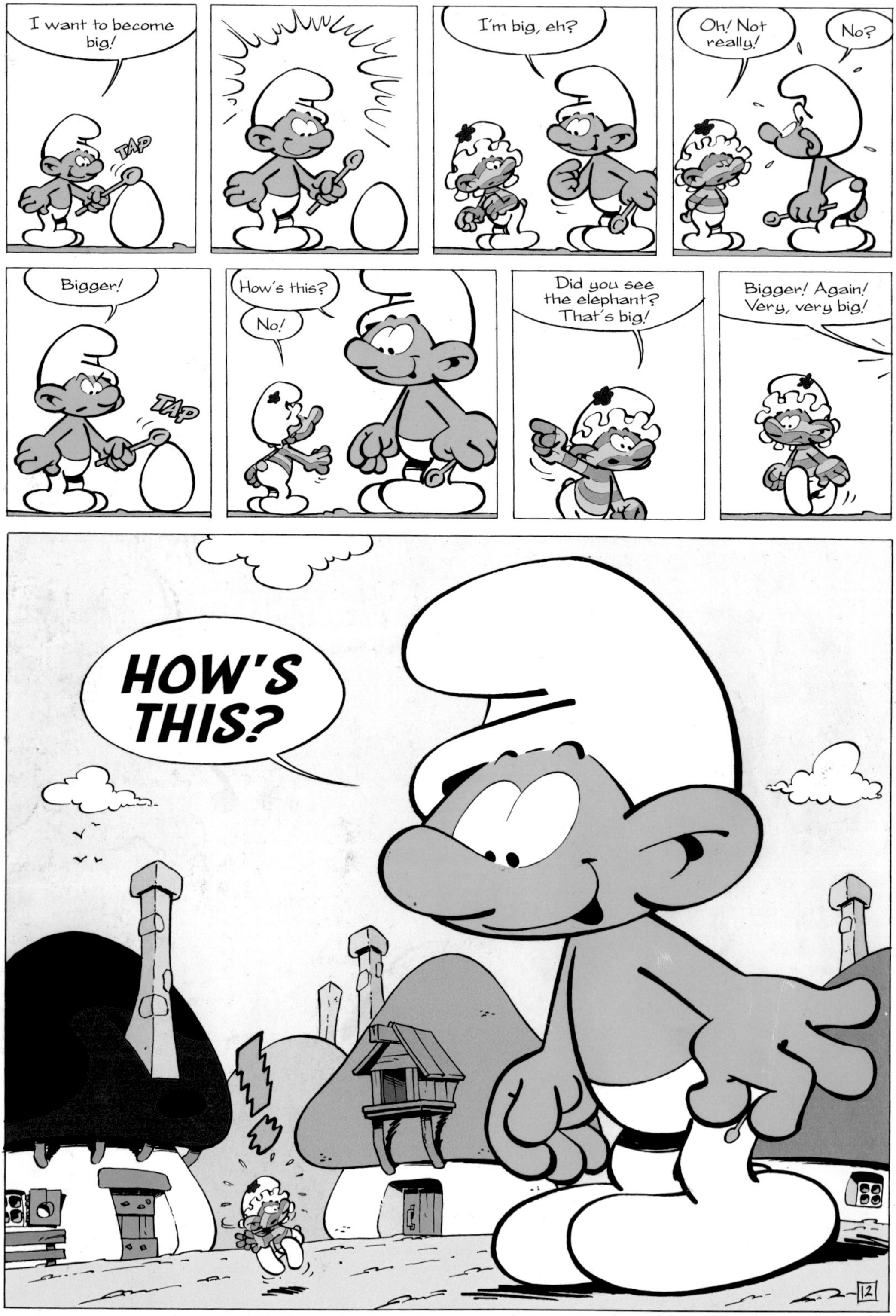
I want to become big!
TAP
I'm big, eh?
Oh! Not really!
No?
Bigger!
TAP
How's this?
No!
Did you see the elephant? That's big!
Bigger! Again! Very, very big!
HOW'S THIS?
12

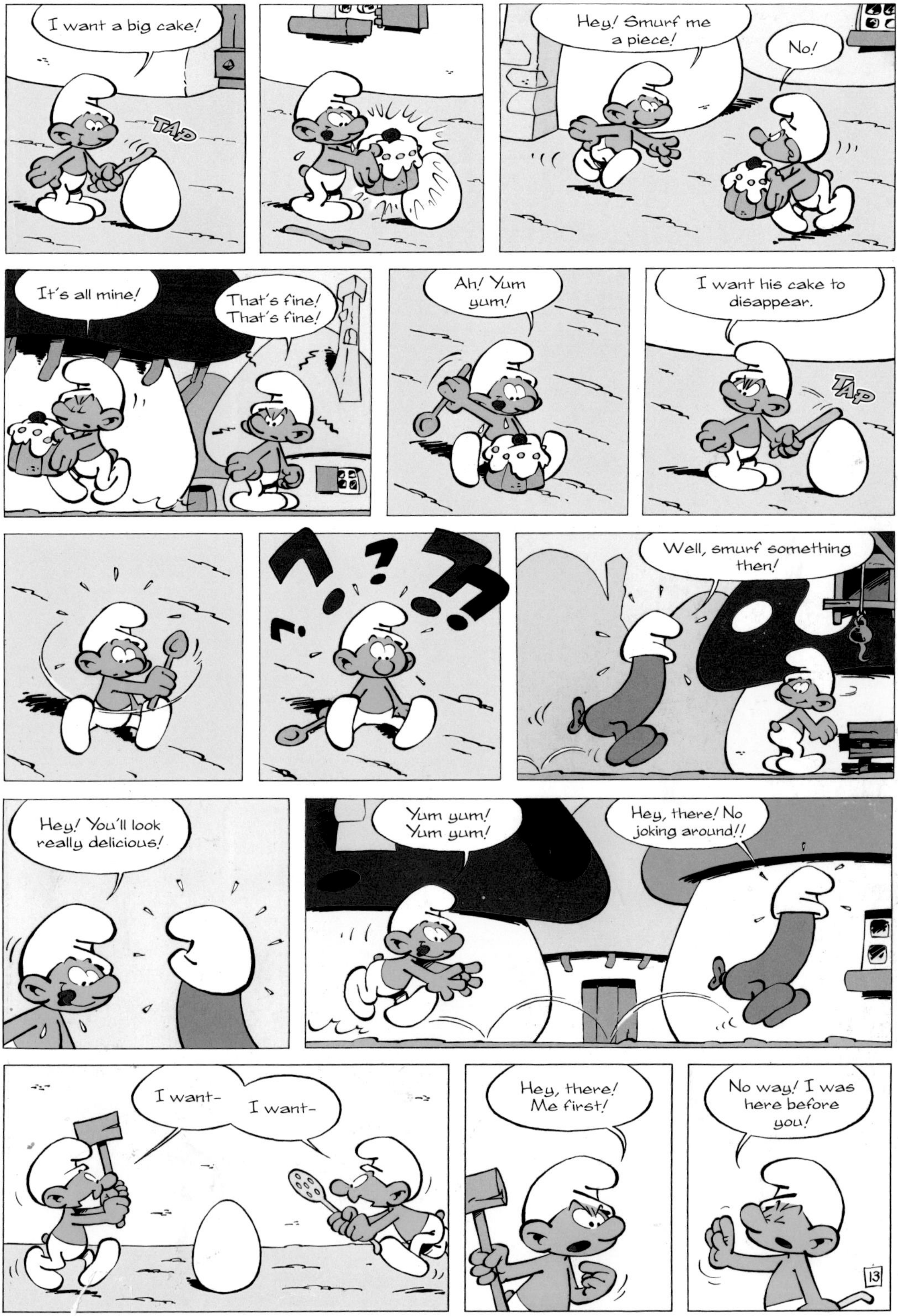
I want a big cake!
TAP
Hey! Smurf me a piece!
No!
It's all mine!
That's fine! That's fine!
Ah! Yum yum!
I want his cake to disappear.
TAP
Well, smurf something then!
Hey! You'll look really delicious!
Yum yum! Yum yum!
Hey, there! No joking around!!
I want-
I want-
Hey, there! Me first!
No way! I was here before you!
13

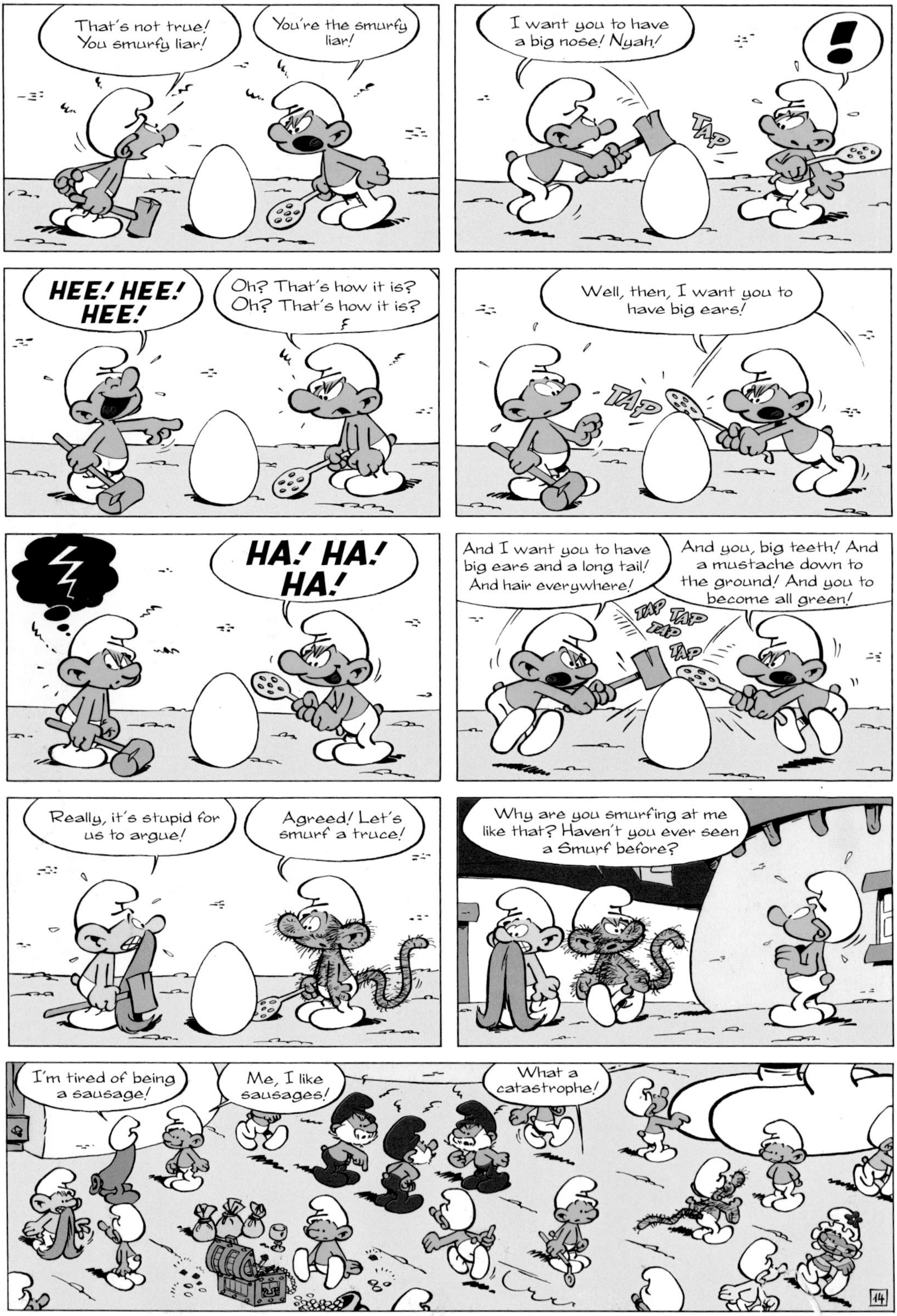
That's not true! You smurfy liar!
You're the smurfy liar!
I want you to have a big nose! Nyah!
TAP
!
HEE! HEE! HEE!
Oh? That's how it is? Oh? That's how it is?
Well, then, I want you to have big ears!
TAP
HA! HA! HA!
And I want you to have big ears and a long tail! And hair everywhere!
And you, big teeth! And a mustache down to the ground! And you to become all green!
TAP TAP TAP TAP
Really, it's stupid for us to argue!
Agreed! Let's smurf a truce!
Why are you smurfing at me like that? Haven't you ever seen a Smurf before?
I'm tired of being a sausage!
Me, I like sausages!
What a catastrophe!
14

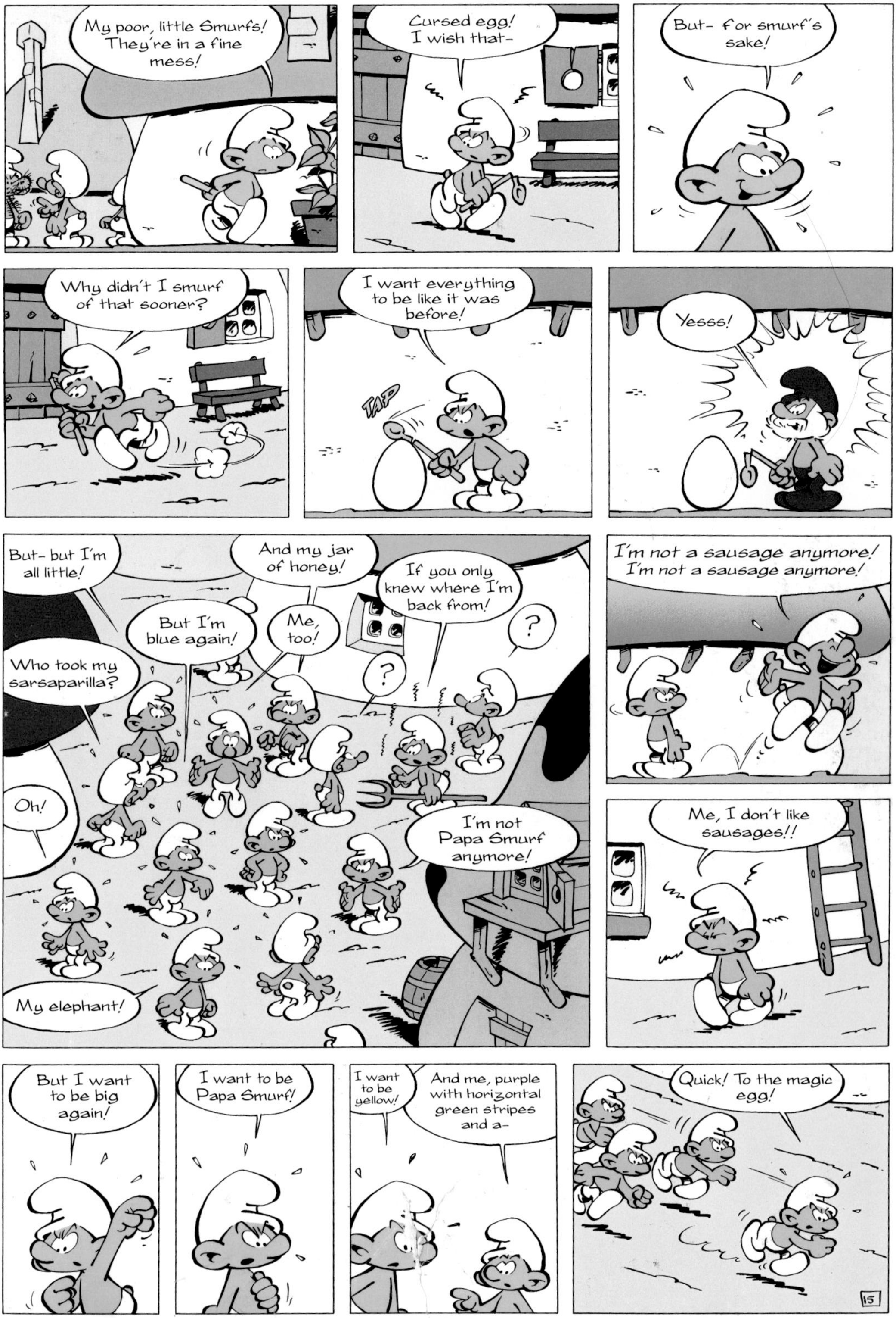
My poor, little Smurfs! They're in a fine mess!
Cursed egg! I wish that-
But- for smurf's sake!
Why didn't I smurf of that sooner?
I want everything to be like it was before!
TAP
Yesss!
But- but I'm all little!
And my jar of honey!
If you only knew where I'm back from!
But I'm blue again!
Me, too!
?
?
Who took my sarsaparilla?
Oh!
I'm not Papa Smurf anymore!
My elephant!
I'm not a sausage anymore! I'm not a sausage anymore!
Me, I don't like sausages!!
But I want to be big again!
I want to be Papa Smurf!
I want to be yellow!
And me, purple with horizontal green stripes and a-
Quick! To the magic egg!
15

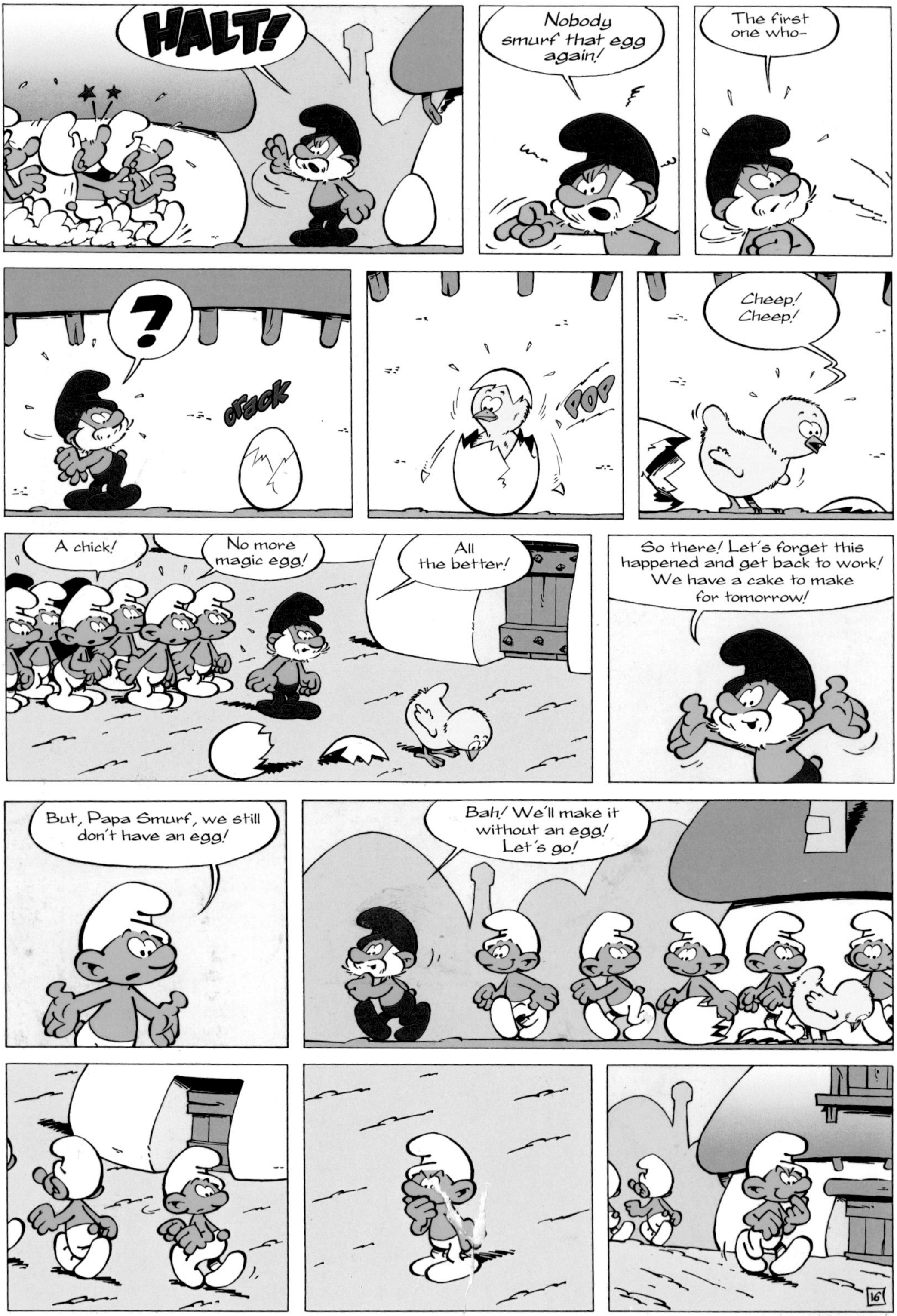
HALT!
Nobody smurf that egg again!
The first one who–
?
CRACK
POP
Cheep! Cheep!
A chick!
No more magic egg!
All the better!
So there! Let's forget this happened and get back to work! We have a cake to make for tomorrow!
But, Papa Smurf, we still don't have an egg!
Bah! We'll make it without an egg! Let's go!
16

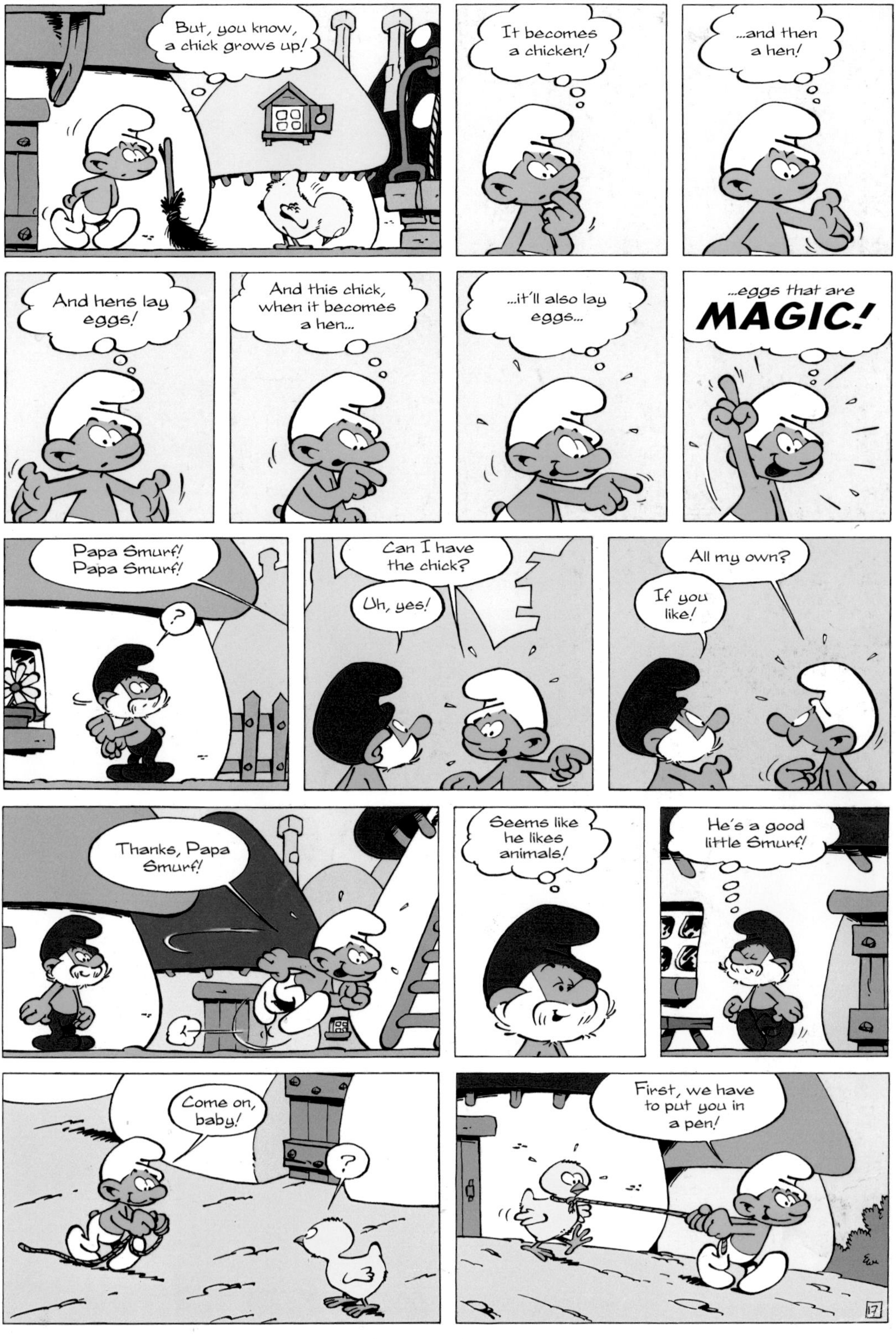
But, you know, a chick grows up!
It becomes a chicken!
...and then a hen!
And hens lay eggs!
And this chick, when it becomes a hen...
...it'll also lay eggs...
...eggs that are MAGIC!
Papa Smurf! Papa Smurf!
?
Can I have the chick?
Uh, yes!
All my own?
If you like!
Thanks, Papa Smurf!
Seems like he likes animals!
He's a good little Smurf!
Come on, baby!
?
First, we have to put you in a pen!
17

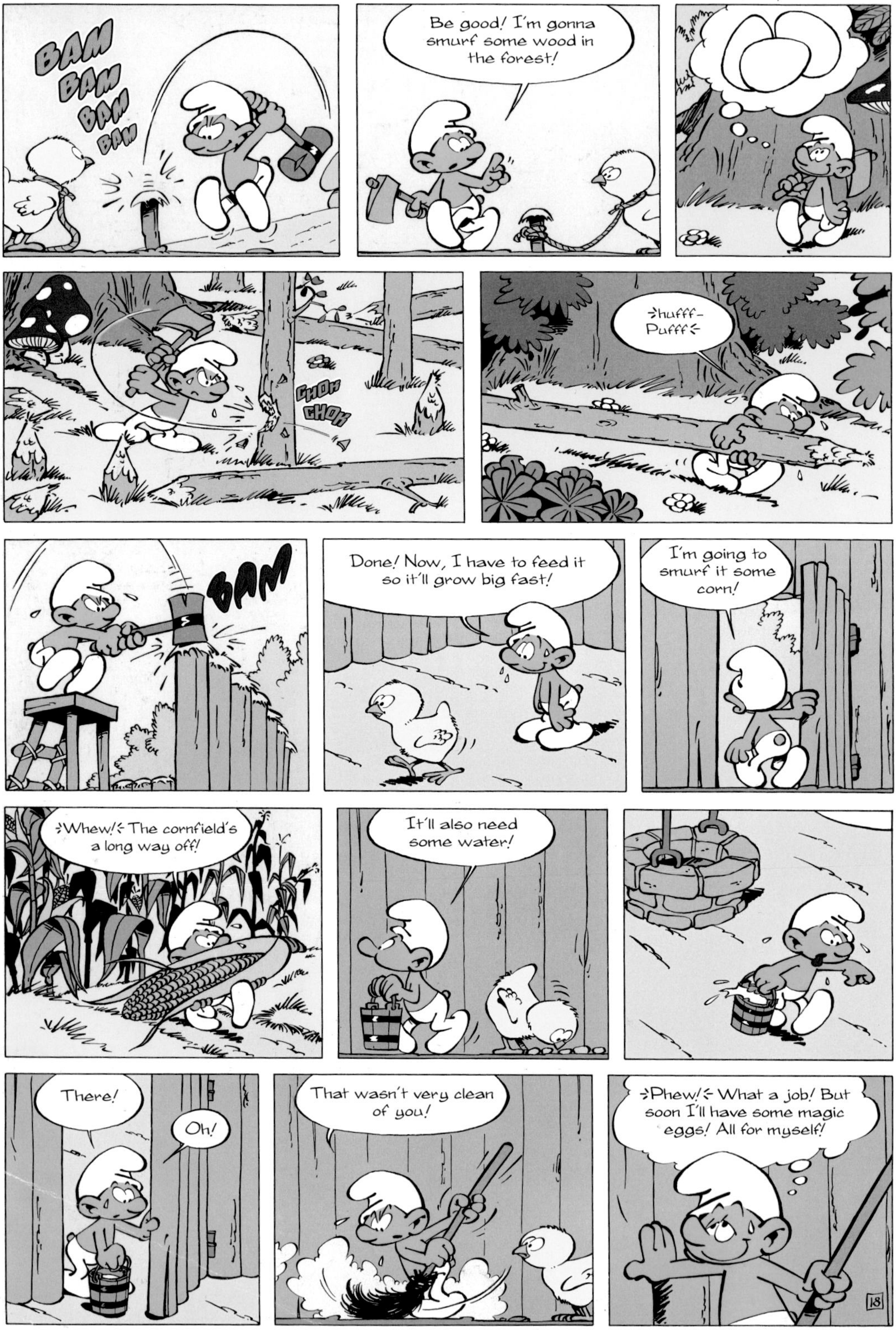
BAM
BAM
BAM
BAM
Be good! I'm gonna smurf some wood in the forest!
CHOK
CHOK
>hufff- Pufff<
BAM
Done! Now, I have to feed it so it'll grow big fast!
I'm going to smurf it some corn!
>Whew!< The cornfield's a long way off!
It'll also need some water!
There!
Oh!
That wasn't very clean of you!
>Phew!< What a job! But soon I'll have some magic eggs! All for myself!
18

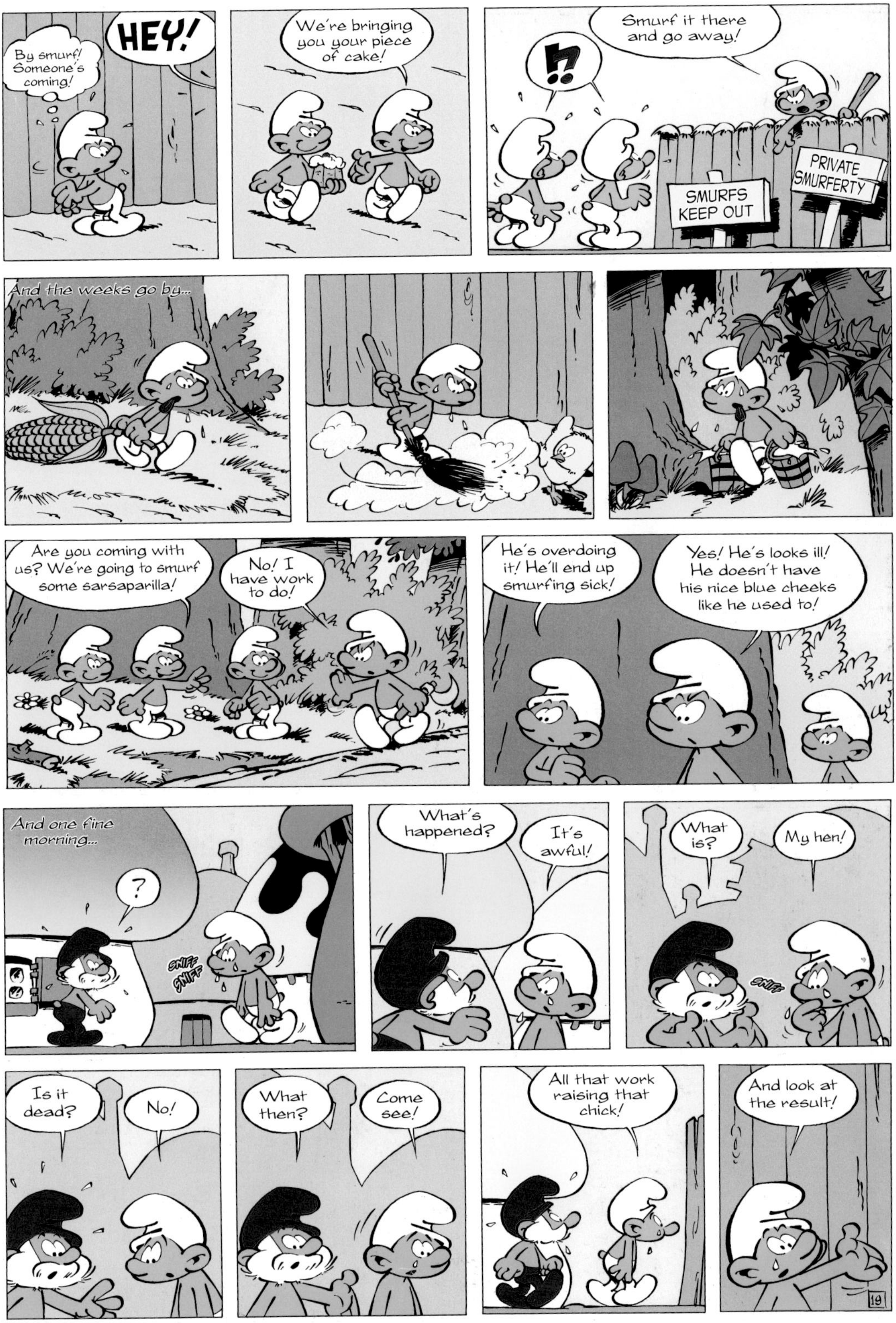
By smurf! Someone's coming!
HEY!
We're bringing you your piece of cake!
!?
Smurf it there and go away!
SMURFS KEEP OUT
PRIVATE SMURFERTY
And the weeks go by...
Are you coming with us? We're going to smurf some sarsaparilla!
No! I have work to do!
He's overdoing it! He'll end up smurfing sick!
Yes! He's looks ill! He doesn't have his nice blue cheeks like he used to!
And one fine morning...
?
SNIFF SNIFF
What's happened?
It's awful!
What is?
My hen!
SNIFF
Is it dead?
No!
What then?
Come see!
All that work raising that chick!
And look at the result!
19

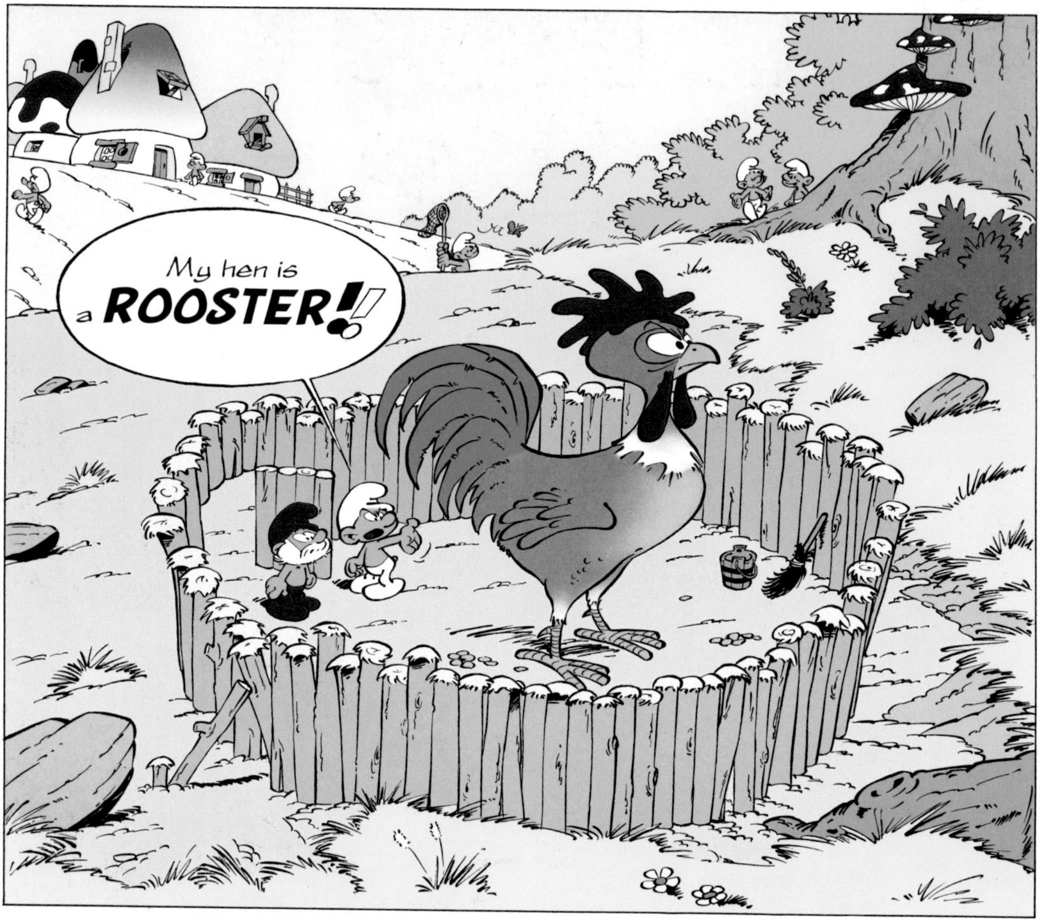
My hen is a ROOSTER!!

THE END

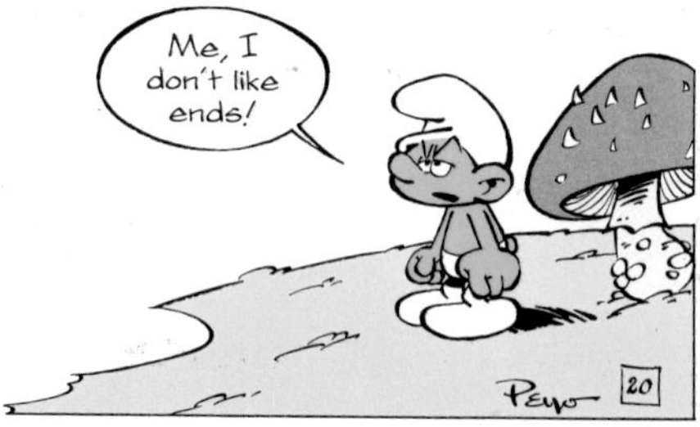
Me, I don't like ends!
PEYO
20

THE FAKE SMURF

by Peyo

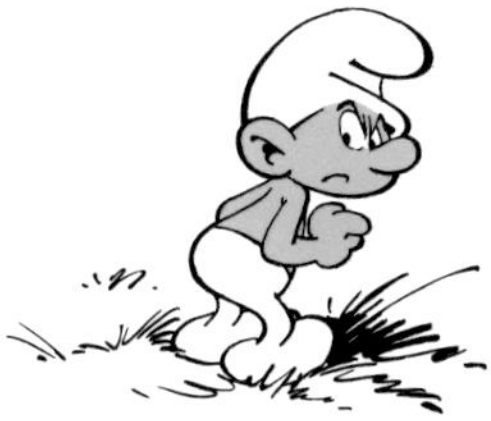

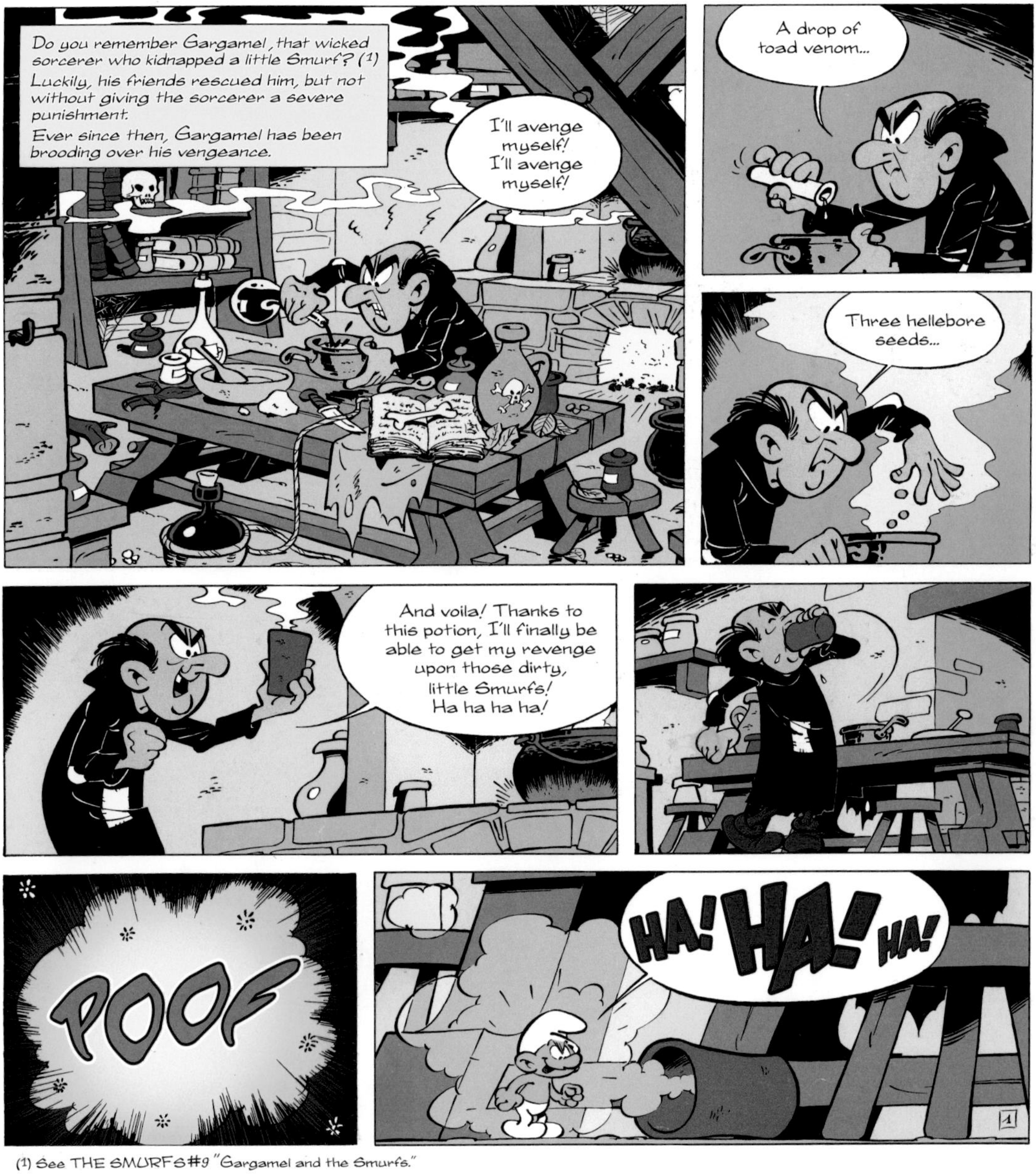

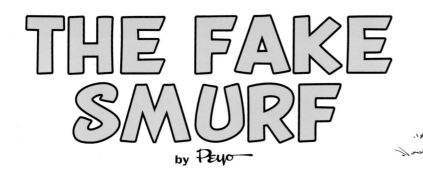

Do you remember Gargamel, that wicked sorcerer who kidnapped a little Smurf? (1) Luckily, his friends rescued him, but not without giving the sorcerer a severe punishment. Ever since then, Gargamel has been brooding over his vengeance.
I'll avenge myself! I'll avenge myself!
A drop of toad venom...
Three hellebore seeds...
And voila! Thanks to this potion, I'll finally be able to get my revenge upon those dirty, little Smurfs! Ha ha ha ha!
POOF
HA! HA! HA!
1

(1) See THE SMURFS #9 "Gargamel and the Smurfs."

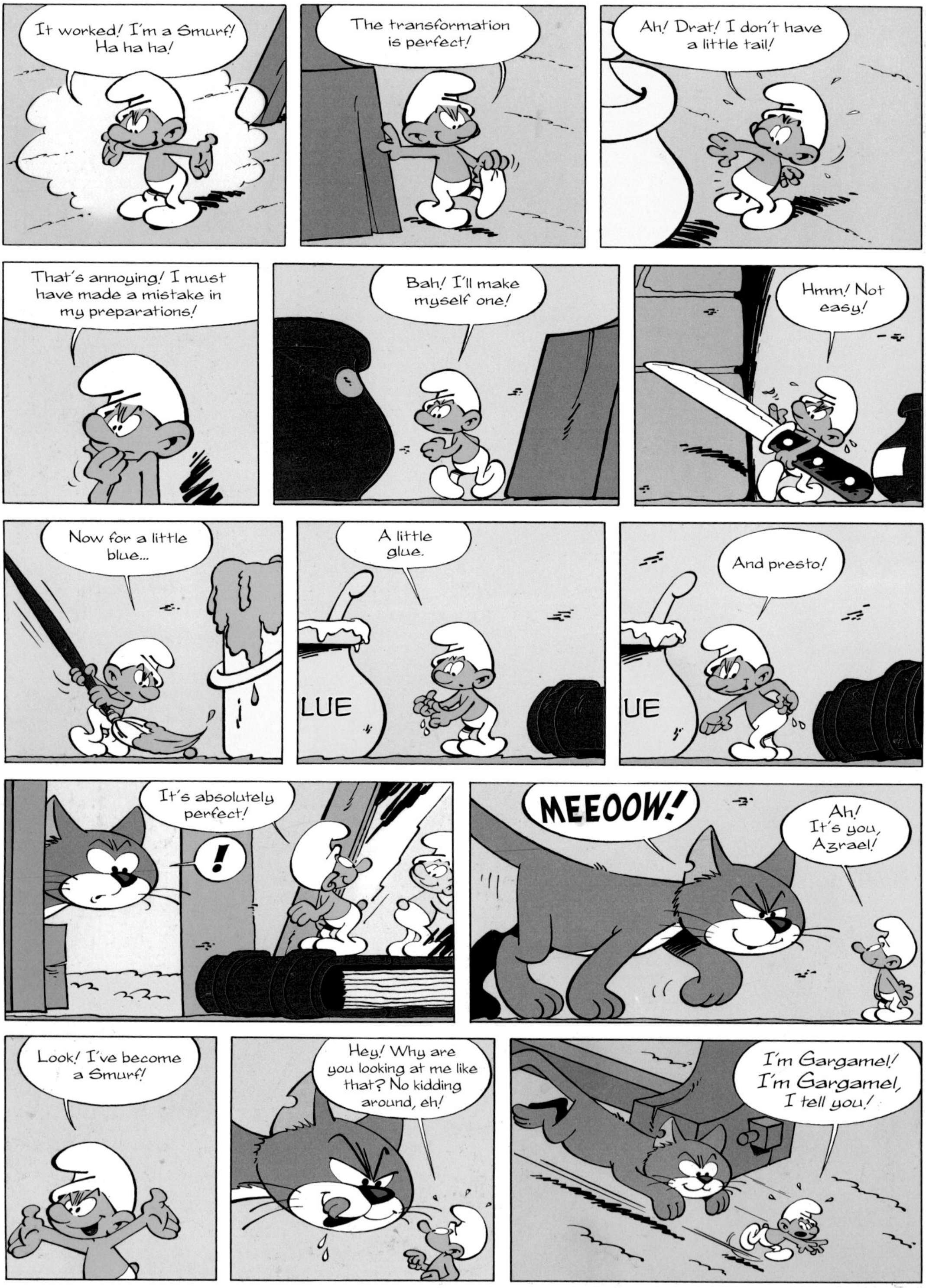
It worked! I'm a Smurf! Ha ha ha!
The transformation is perfect!
Ah! Drat! I don't have a little tail!
That's annoying! I must have made a mistake in my preparations!
Bah! I'll make myself one!
Hmm! Not easy!
Now for a little blue...
A little glue.
LUE
And presto!
UE
It's absolutely perfect!
!
MEEOOW!
Ah! It's you, Azrael!
Look! I've become a Smurf!
Hey! Why are you looking at me like that? No kidding around, eh!
I'm Gargamel! I'm Gargamel, I tell you!

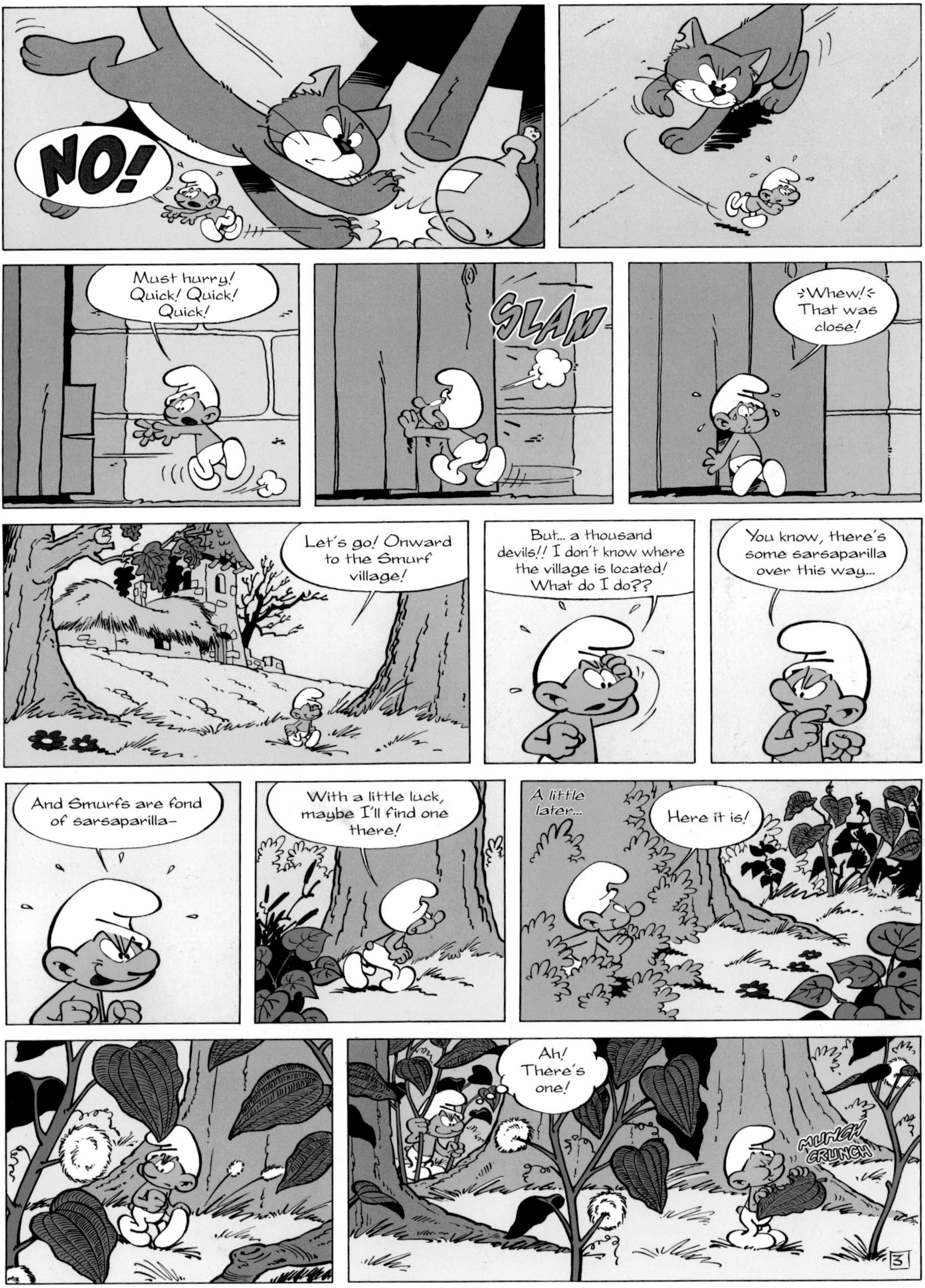
NO!
Must hurry! Quick! Quick! Quick!
SLAM
Whew! That was close!
Let's go! Onward to the Smurf village!
But... a thousand devils!! I don't know where the village is located! What do I do??
You know, there's some sarsaparilla over this way...
And Smurfs are fond of sarsaparilla–
With a little luck, maybe I'll find one there!
A little later...
Here it is!
Ah! There's one!
MUNCH
CRUNCH
3

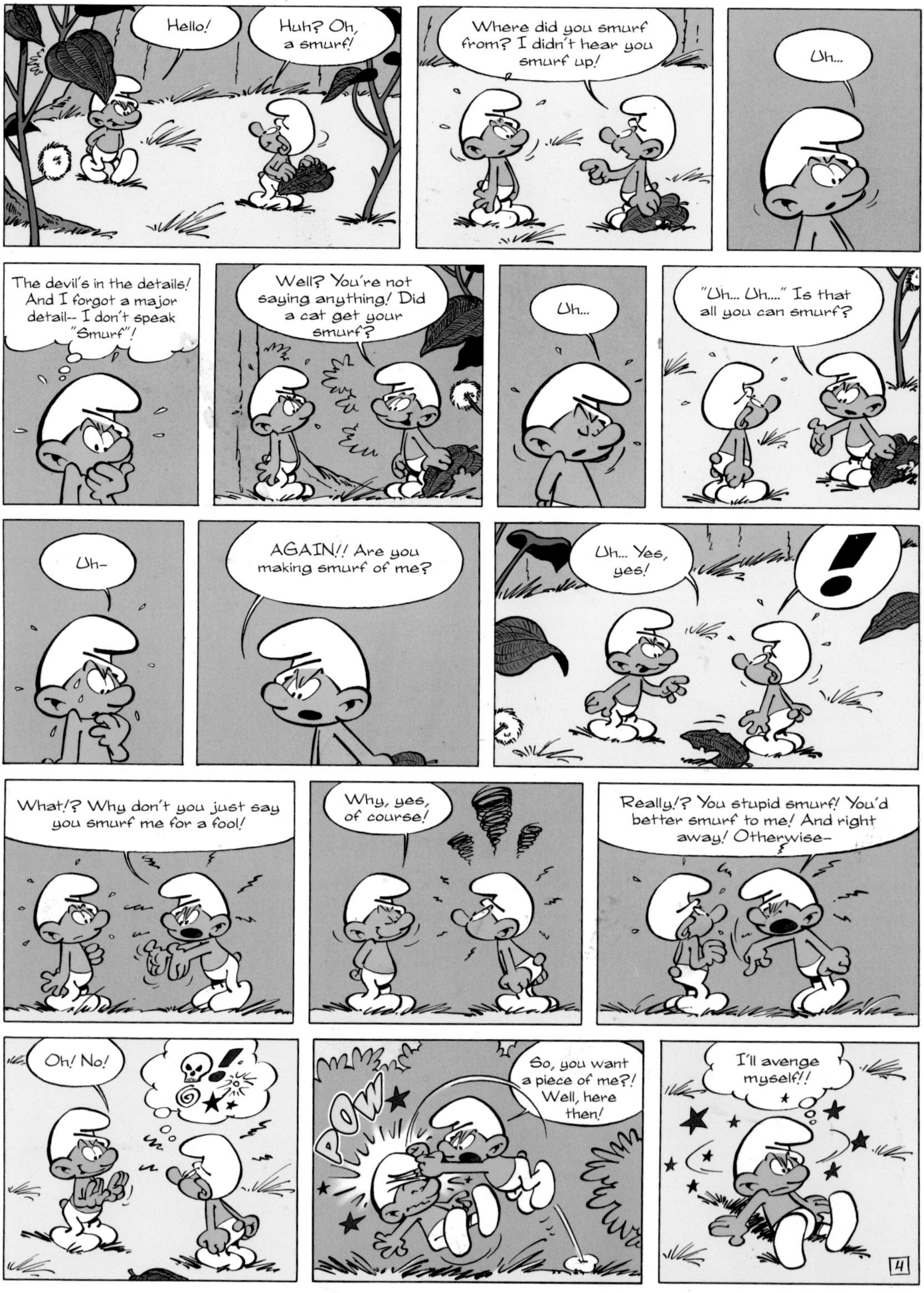

Hello!
Huh? Oh, a smurf!
Where did you smurf from? I didn't hear you smurf up!
Uh...
The devil's in the details! And I forgot a major detail-- I don't speak "Smurf"!
Well? You're not saying anything! Did a cat get your smurf?
Uh...
"Uh... Uh...." Is that all you can smurf?
Uh-
AGAIN!! Are you making smurf of me?
Uh... Yes, yes!
!
What!? Why don't you just say you smurf me for a fool!
Why, yes, of course!
Really!? You stupid smurf! You'd better smurf to me! And right away! Otherwise-
Oh! No!
POW
So, you want a piece of me?! Well, here then!
I'll avenge myself!!
4

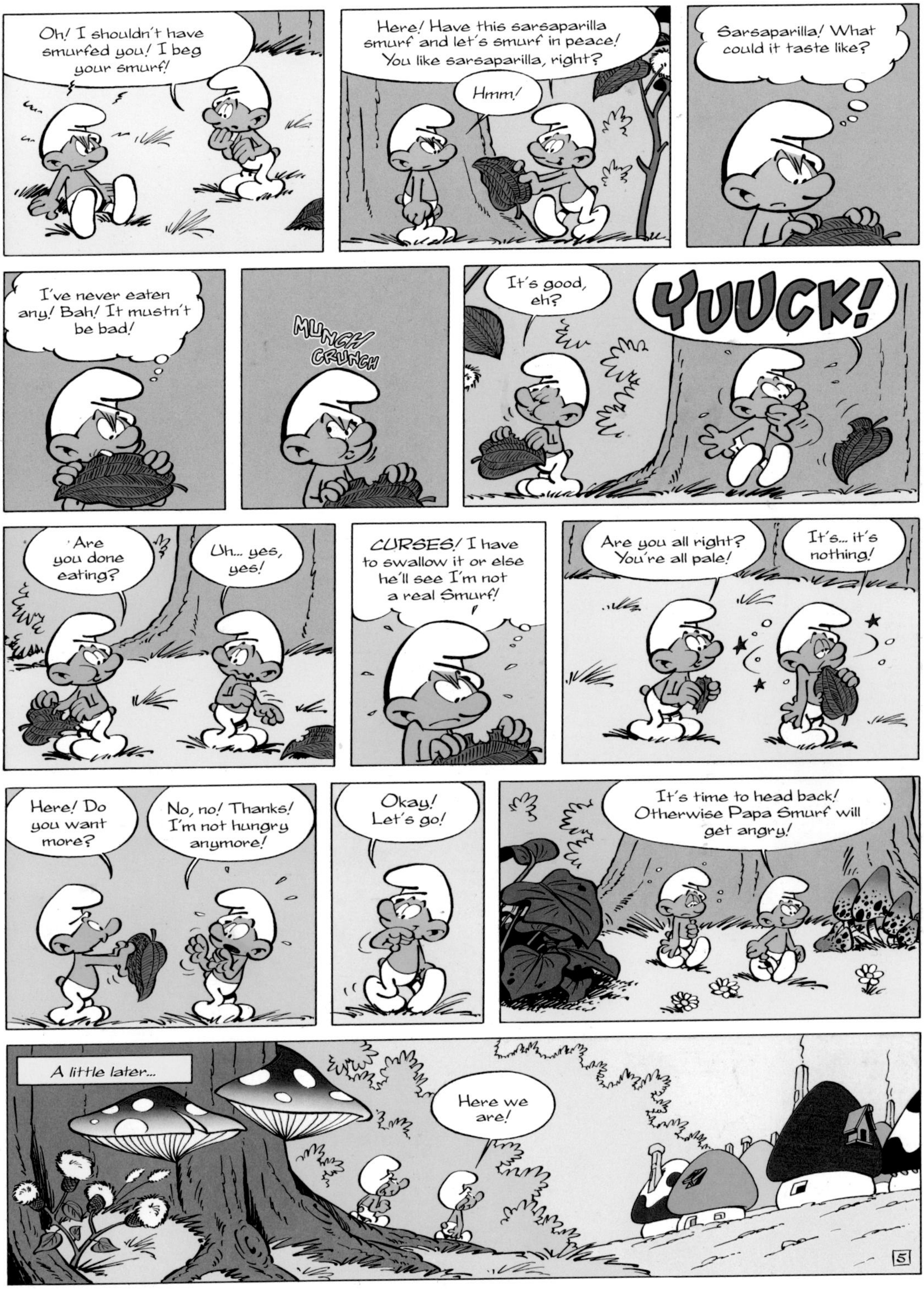
Oh! I shouldn't have smurfed you! I beg your smurf!
Here! Have this sarsaparilla smurf and let's smurf in peace! You like sarsaparilla, right?
Hmm!
Sarsaparilla! What could it taste like?
I've never eaten any! Bah! It mustn't be bad!
MUNCH CRUNCH
It's good, eh?
YUUCK!
Are you done eating?
Uh... yes, yes!
CURSES! I have to swallow it or else he'll see I'm not a real Smurf!
Are you all right? You're all pale!
It's... it's nothing!
Here! Do you want more?
No, no! Thanks! I'm not hungry anymore!
Okay! Let's go!
It's time to head back! Otherwise Papa Smurf will get angry!
A little later...
Here we are!
5

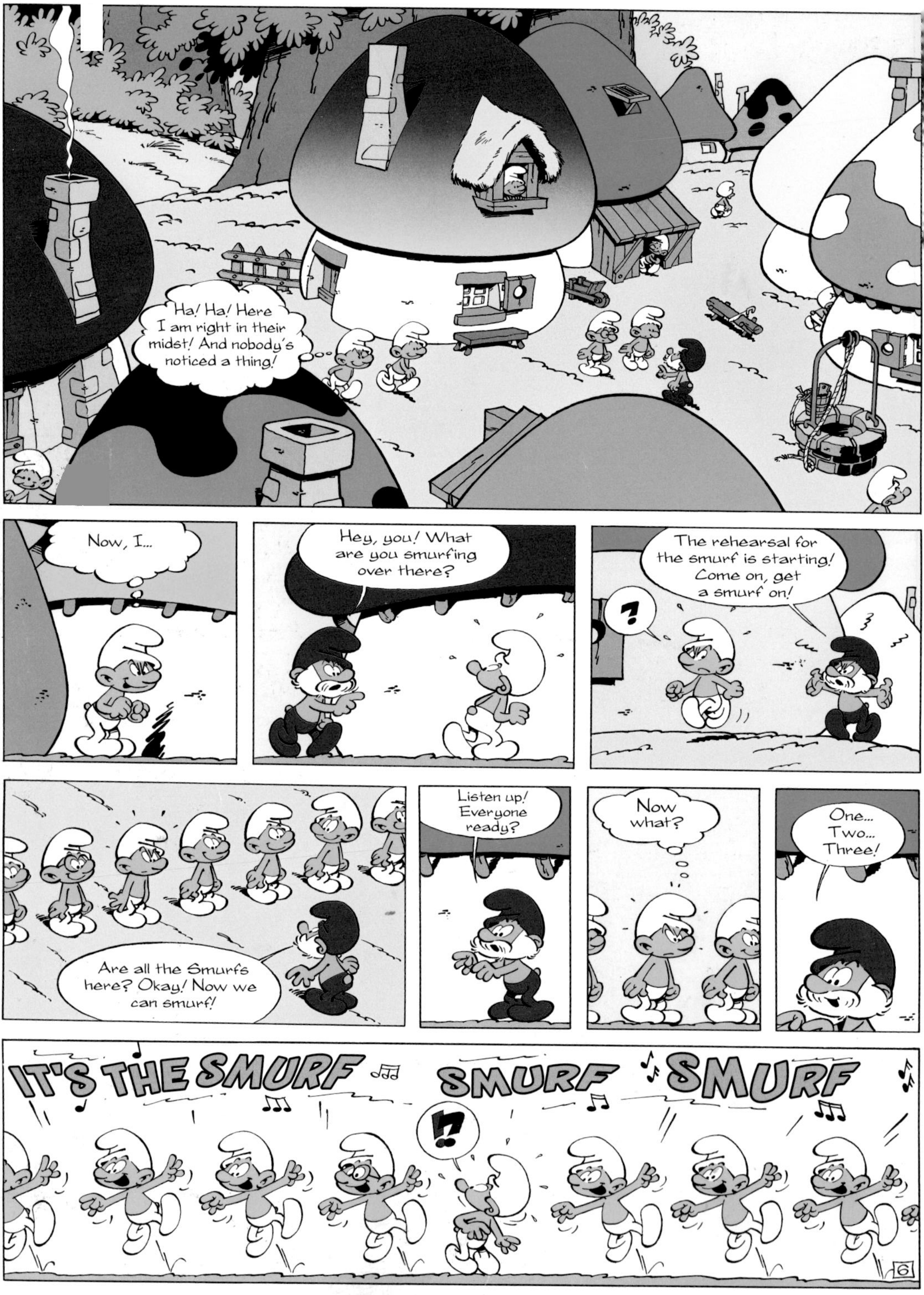
Ha! Ha! Here I am right in their midst! And nobody's noticed a thing!
Now, I...
Hey, you! What are you smurfing over there?
?
The rehearsal for the smurf is starting! Come on, get a smurf on!
Are all the Smurfs here? Okay! Now we can smurf!
Listen up! Everyone ready?
Now what?
One... Two... Three!
IT'S THE SMURF SMURF SMURF
!?
6

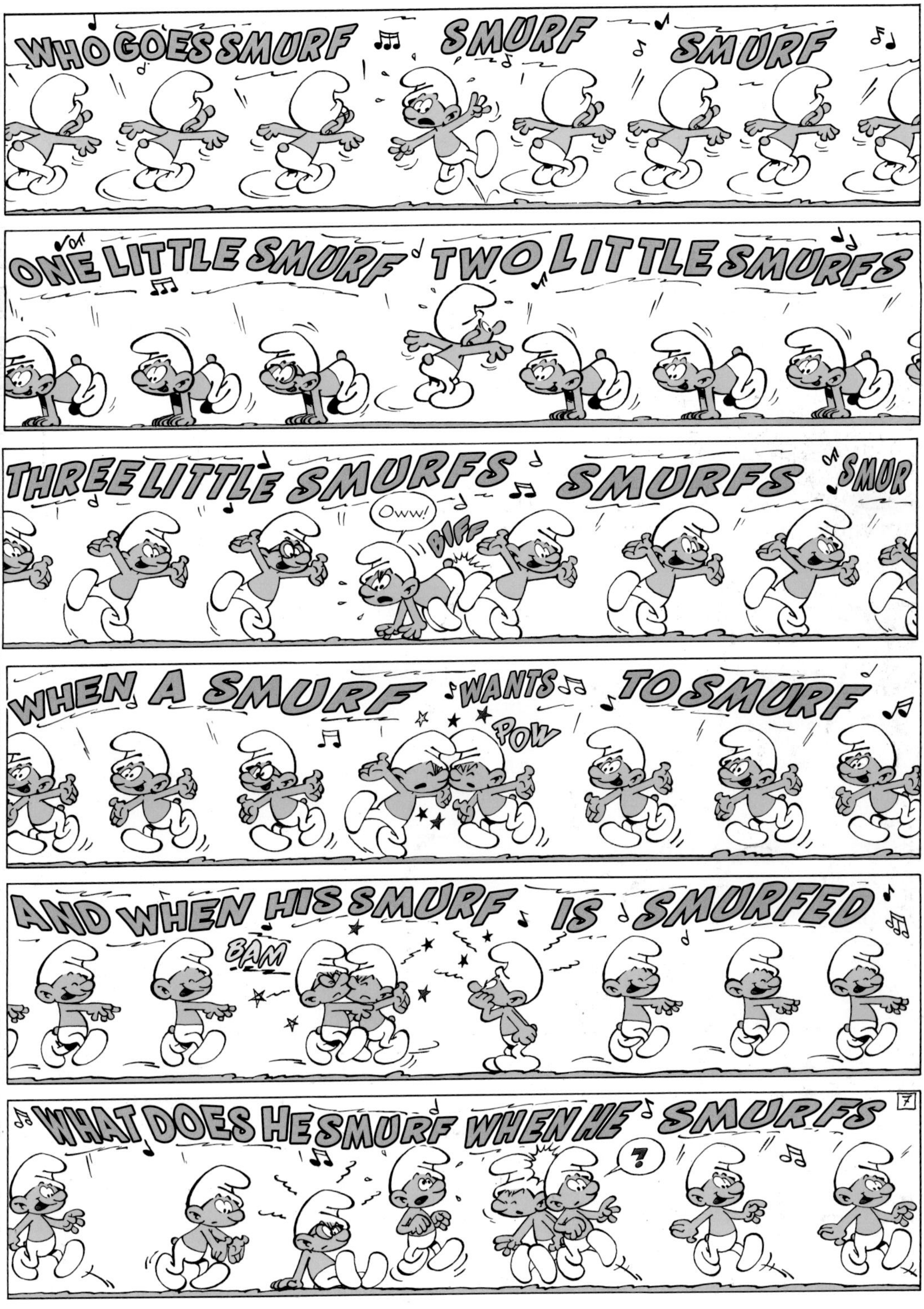
WHO GOES SMURF
SMURF
SMURF
ONE LITTLE SMURF
TWO LITTLE SMURFS
THREE LITTLE SMURFS
SMURFS
SMUR
OWW!
BIFF
WHEN A SMURF
WANTS
TO SMURF
POW
AND WHEN HIS SMURF
IS
SMURFED
BAM
WHAT DOES HE SMURF WHEN HE
SMURFS
7
?

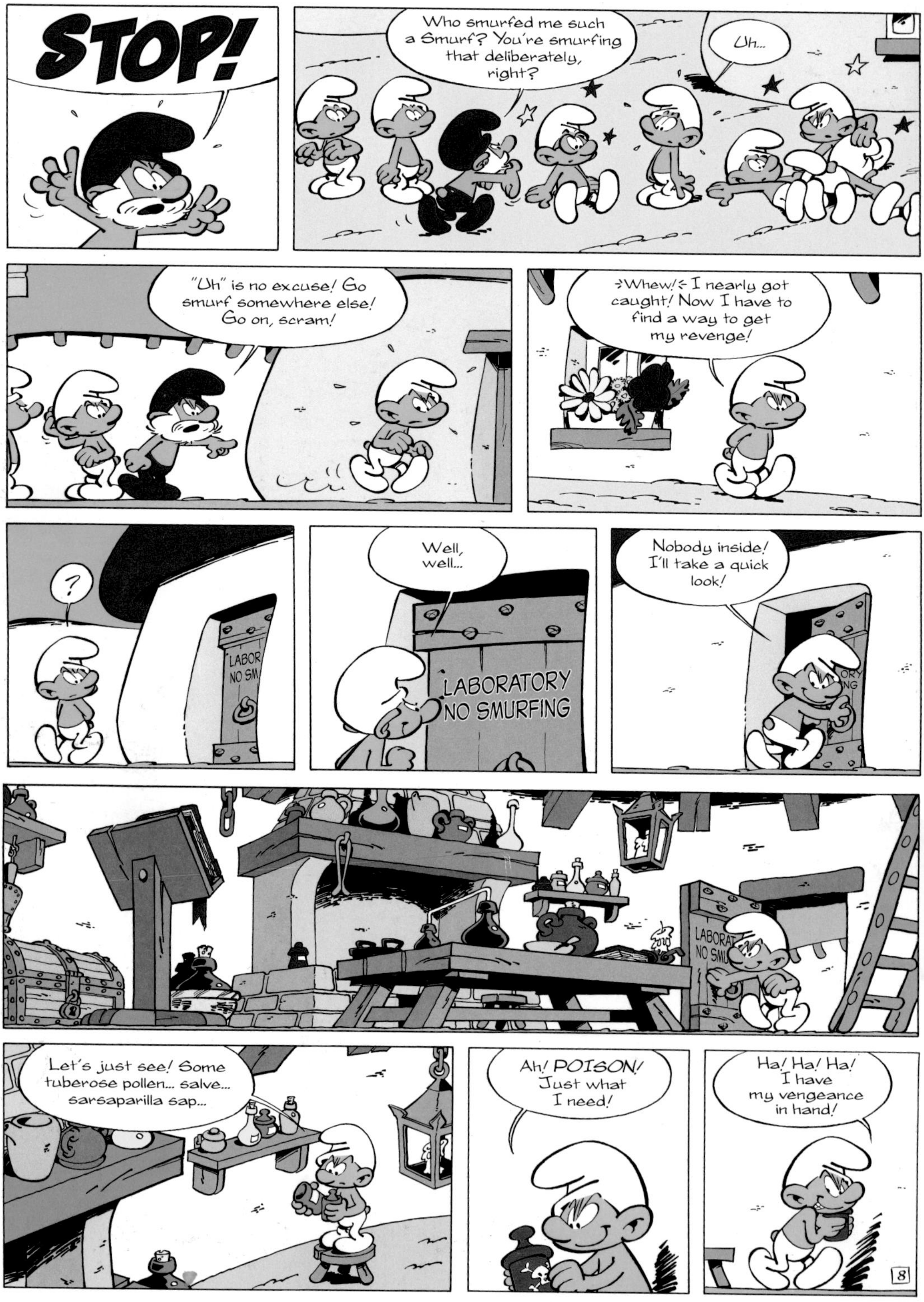
STOP!
Who smurfed me such a Smurf? You're smurfing that deliberately, right?
Uh...
"Uh" is no excuse! Go smurf somewhere else! Go on, scram!
Whew! I nearly got caught! Now I have to find a way to get my revenge!
?
Well, well...
LABORATORY NO SMURFING
Nobody inside! I'll take a quick look!
Let's just see! Some tuberose pollen... salve... sarsaparilla sap...
Ah! POISON! Just what I need!
Ha! Ha! Ha! I have my vengeance in hand!
8

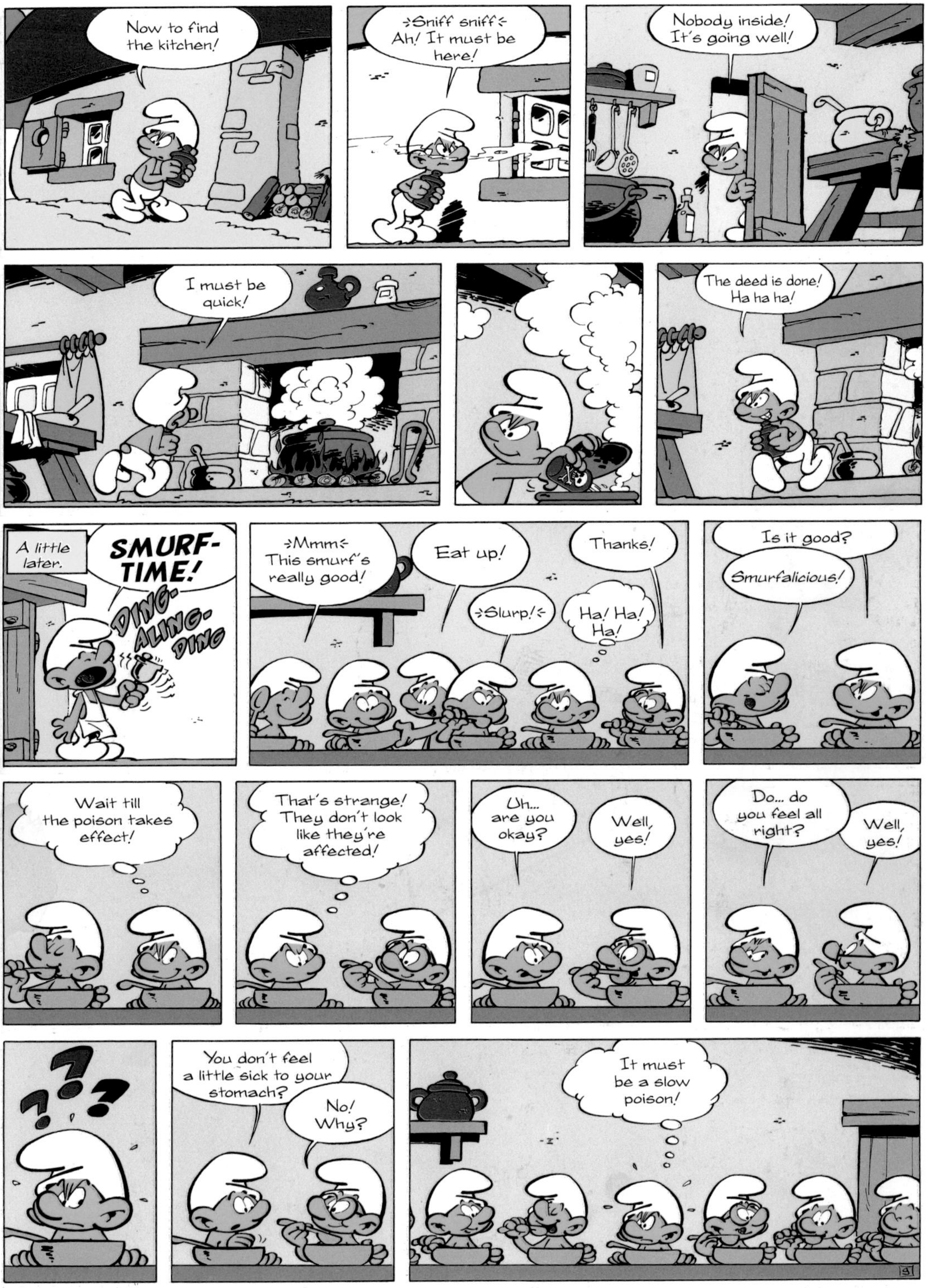

Now to find the kitchen!
-Sniff sniff- Ah! It must be here!
Nobody inside! It's going well!
I must be quick!
The deed is done! Ha ha ha!
A little later.
SMURF-TIME!
DING-ALING-DING
-Mmm- This smurf's really good!
Eat up!
-Slurp!-
Thanks!
Ha! Ha! Ha!
Is it good?
Smurfalicious!
Wait till the poison takes effect!
That's strange! They don't look like they're affected!
Uh... are you okay?
Well, yes!
Do... do you feel all right?
Well, yes!
You don't feel a little sick to your stomach?
No! Why?
It must be a slow poison!

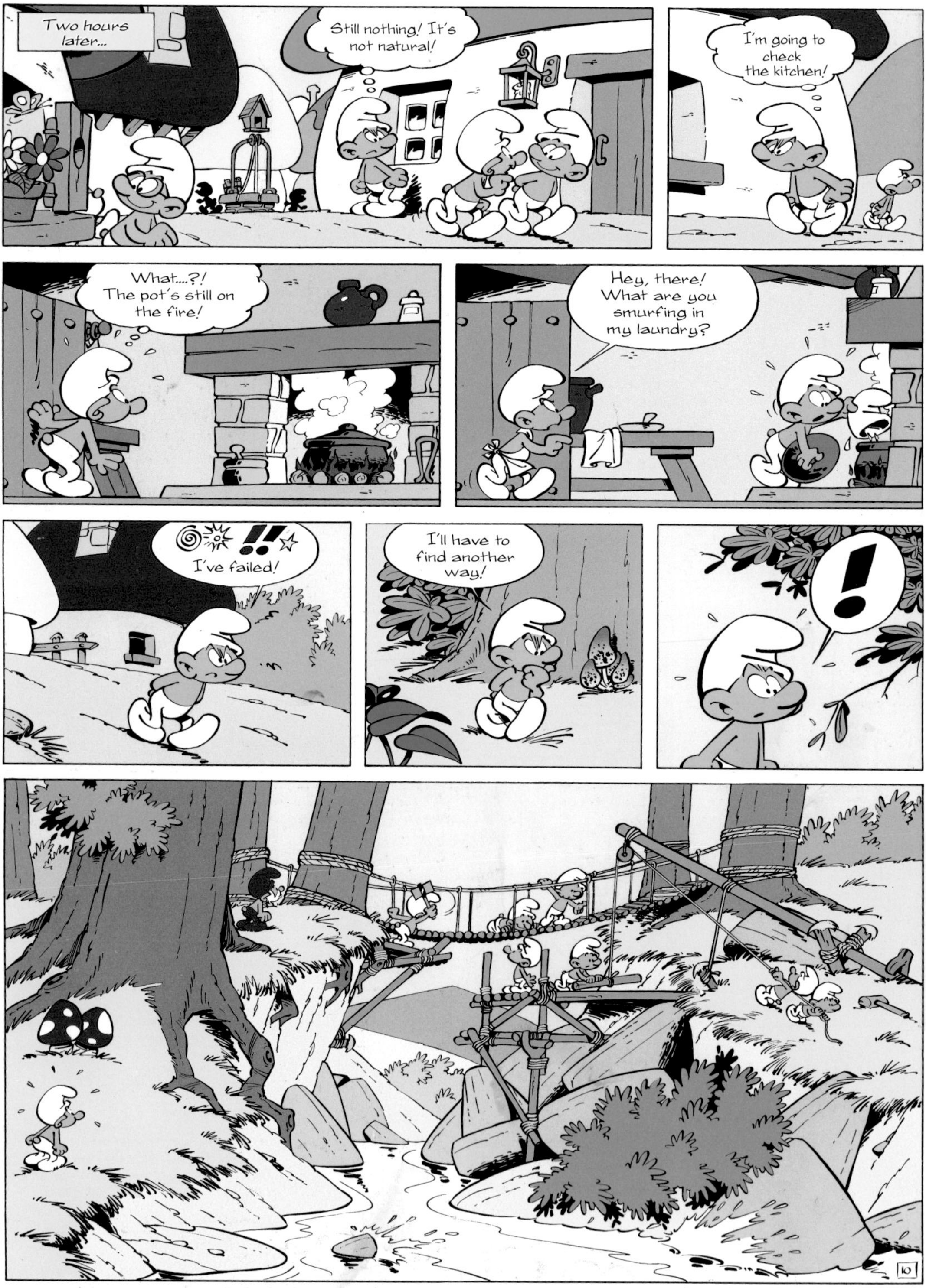
Two hours later...
Still nothing! It's not natural!
I'm going to check the kitchen!
What...?! The pot's still on the fire!
Hey, there! What are you smurfing in my laundry?
I've failed!
I'll have to find another way!
!
10

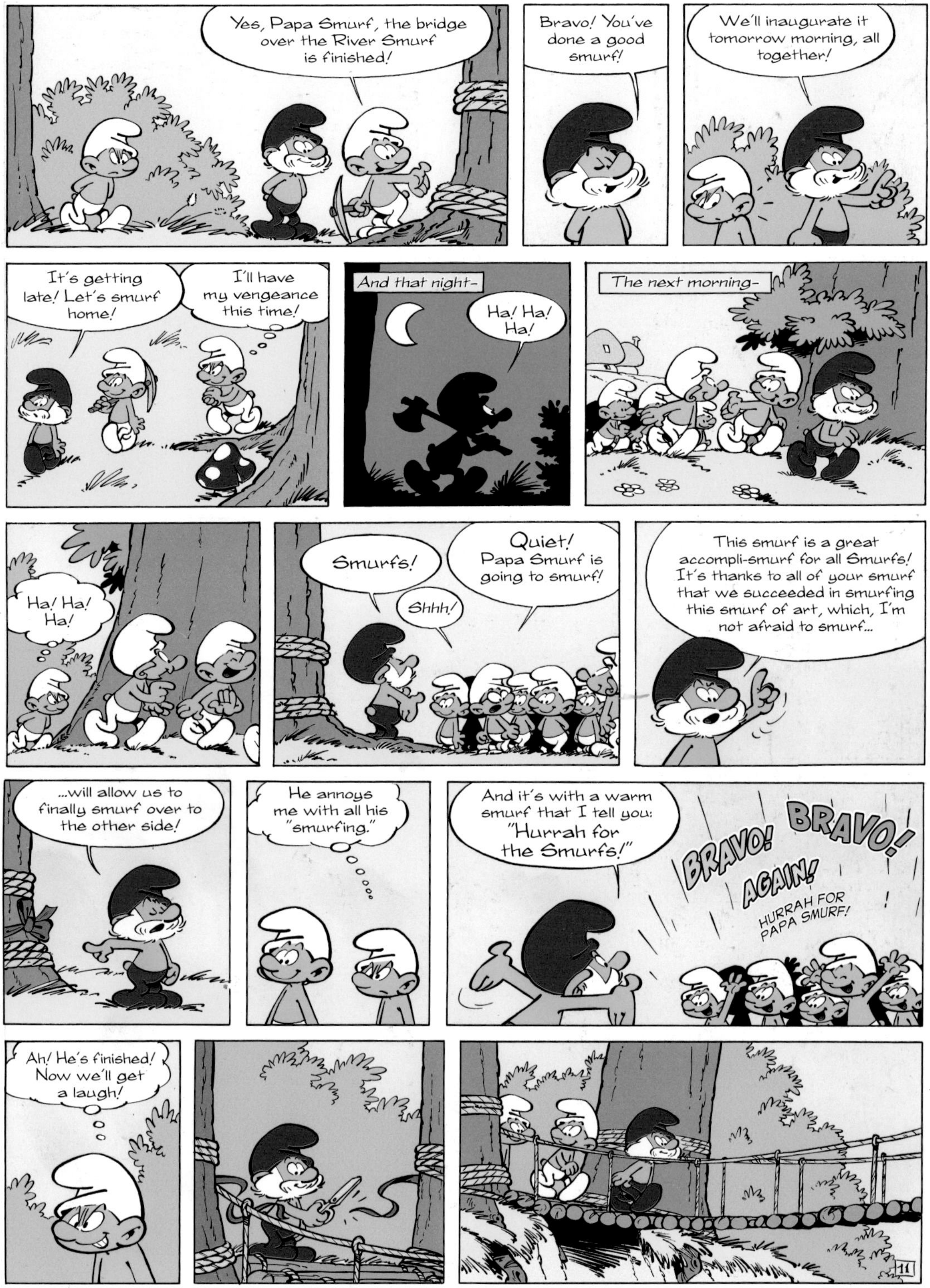

Yes, Papa Smurf, the bridge over the River Smurf is finished!
Bravo! You've done a good smurf!
We'll inaugurate it tomorrow morning, all together!
It's getting late! Let's smurf home!
I'll have my vengeance this time!
And that night-
Ha! Ha! Ha!
The next morning-
Ha! Ha! Ha!
Smurfs!
Shhh!
Quiet! Papa Smurf is going to smurf!
This smurf is a great accompli-smurf for all Smurfs! It's thanks to all of your smurf that we succeeded in smurfing this smurf of art, which, I'm not afraid to smurf...
...will allow us to finally smurf over to the other side!
He annoys me with all his "smurfing."
And it's with a warm smurf that I tell you: "Hurrah for the Smurfs!"
BRAVO!
BRAVO!
AGAIN!
HURRAH FOR PAPA SMURF!
Ah! He's finished! Now we'll get a laugh!
11

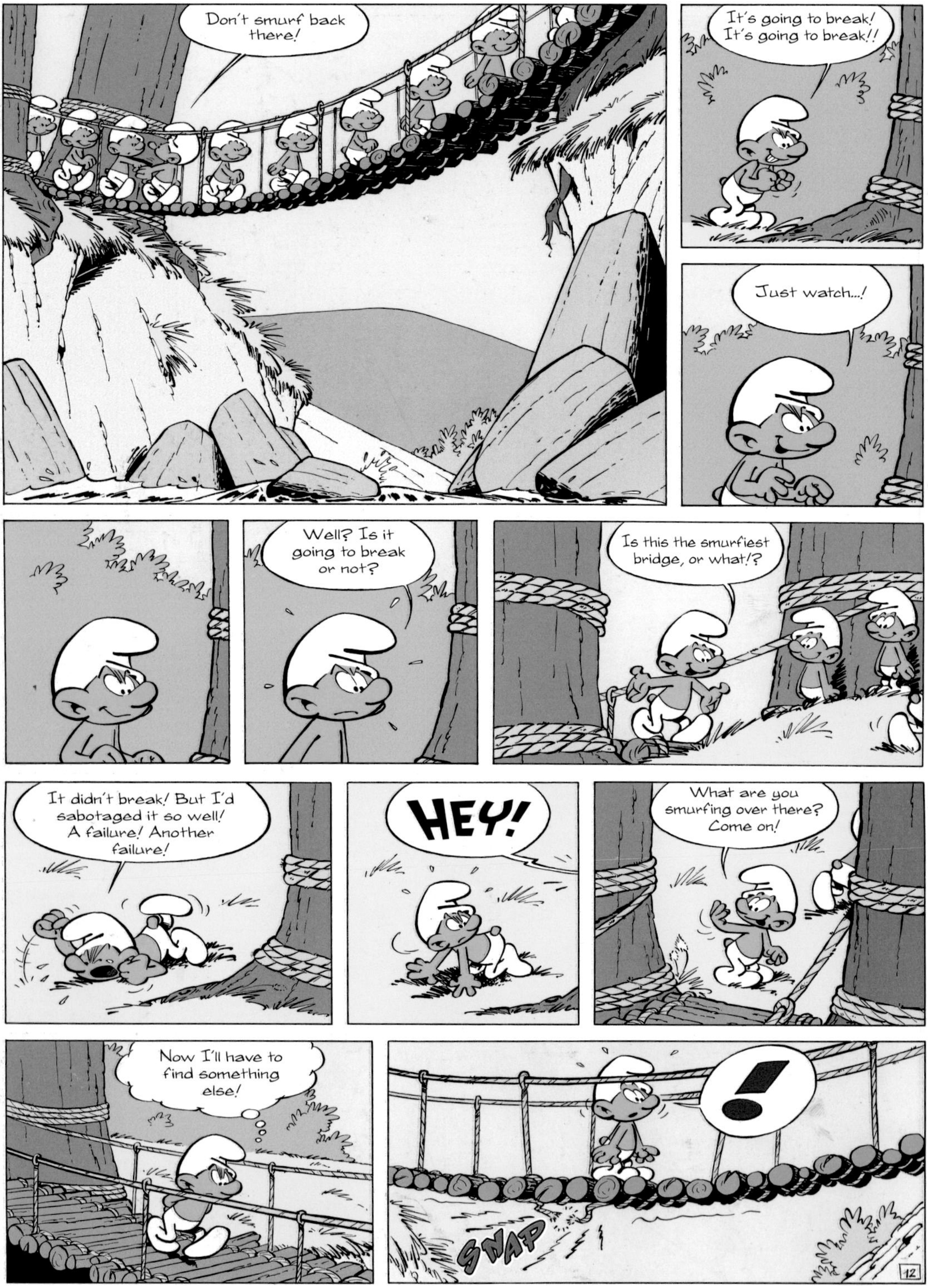
Don't smurf back there!
It's going to break! It's going to break!!
Just watch...!
Well? Is it going to break or not?
Is this the smurfiest bridge, or what!?
It didn't break! But I'd sabotaged it so well! A failure! Another failure!
HEY!
What are you smurfing over there? Come on!
Now I'll have to find something else!
!
SNAP
12

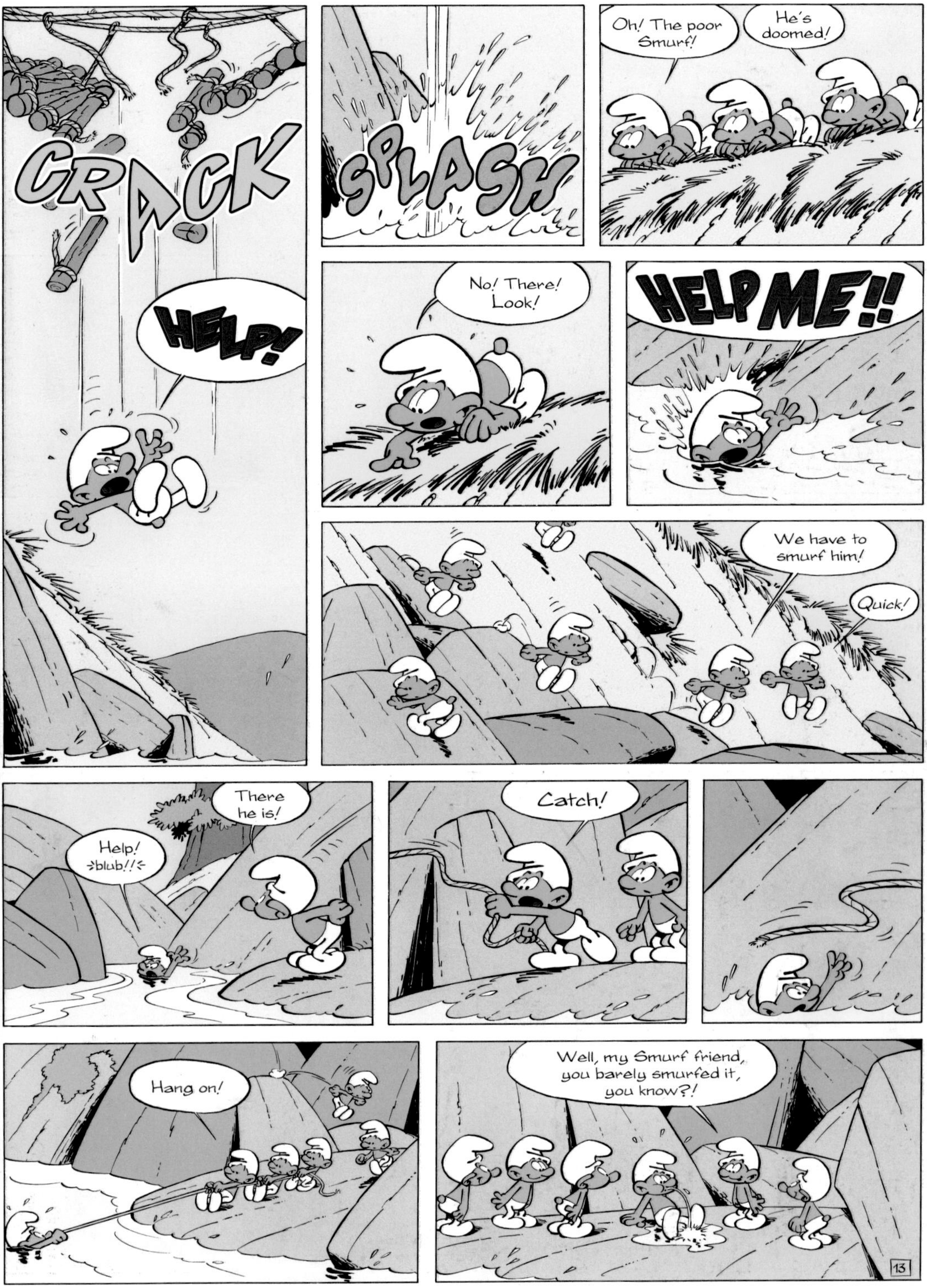
CRACK
HELP!
SPLASH
Oh! The poor Smurf!
He's doomed!
No! There! Look!
HELP ME!!
We have to smurf him!
Quick!
There he is!
Help! blub!!
Catch!
Hang on!
Well, my Smurf friend, you barely smurfed it, you know?!
13

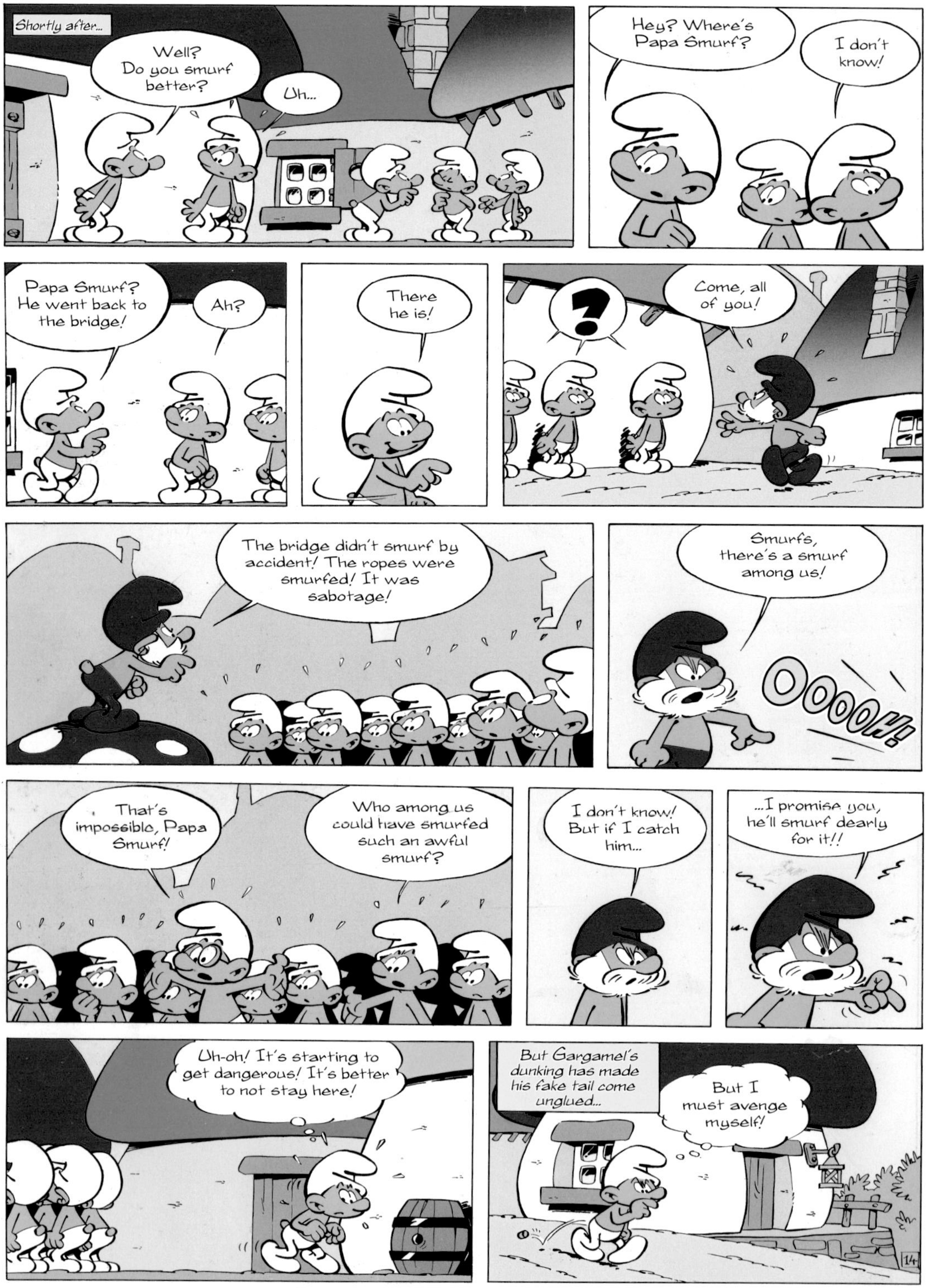

Shortly after...
Well? Do you smurf better?
Uh...
Hey? Where's Papa Smurf?
I don't know!
Papa Smurf? He went back to the bridge!
Ah?
There he is!
?
Come, all of you!
The bridge didn't smurf by accident! The ropes were smurfed! It was sabotage!
Smurfs, there's a smurf among us!
OOOOH!
That's impossible, Papa Smurf!
Who among us could have smurfed such an awful smurf?
I don't know! But if I catch him...
...I promise you, he'll smurf dearly for it!!
Uh-oh! It's starting to get dangerous! It's better to not stay here!
But Gargamel's dunking has made his fake tail come unglued...
But I must avenge myself!

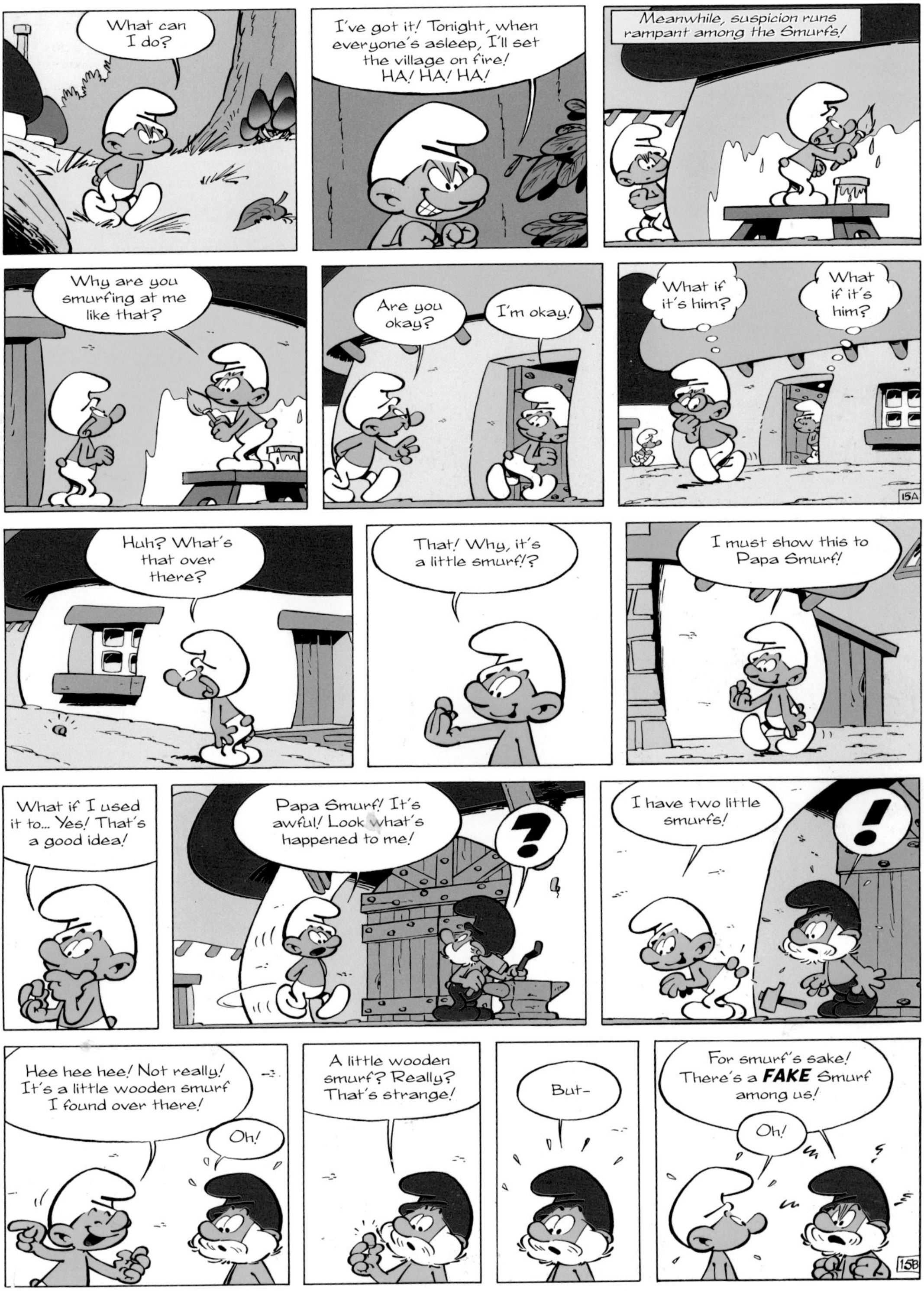
What can I do?
I've got it! Tonight, when everyone's asleep, I'll set the village on fire! HA! HA! HA!
Meanwhile, suspicion runs rampant among the Smurfs!
Why are you smurfing at me like that?
Are you okay?
I'm okay!
What if it's him?
What if it's him?
15A
Huh? What's that over there?
That! Why, it's a little smurf!?
I must show this to Papa Smurf!
What if I used it to... Yes! That's a good idea!
Papa Smurf! It's awful! Look what's happened to me!
?
I have two little smurfs!
!
Hee hee hee! Not really! It's a little wooden smurf I found over there!
Oh!
A little wooden smurf? Really? That's strange!
But-
For smurf's sake! There's a FAKE Smurf among us!
Oh!
15B

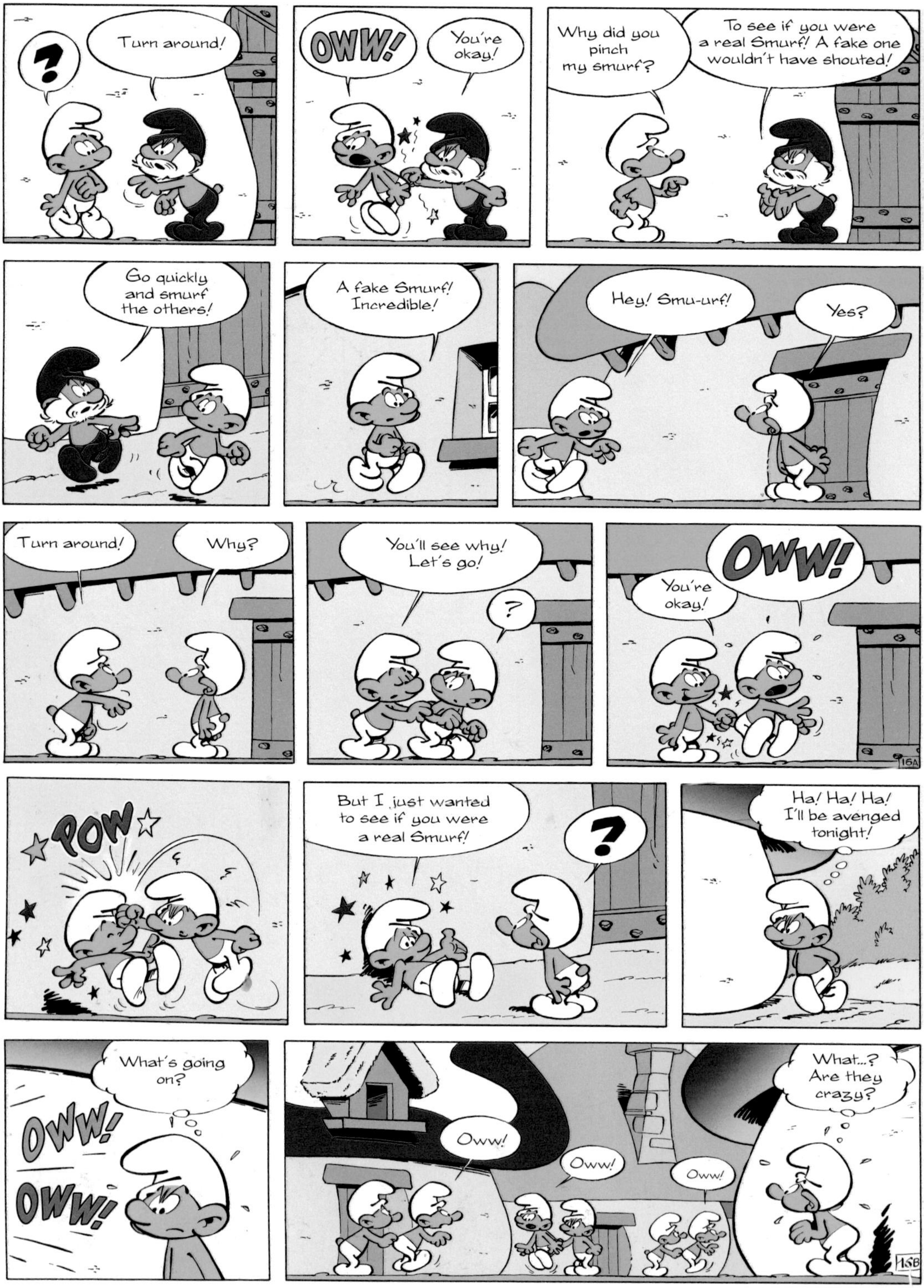
?
Turn around!
OWW!
You're okay!
Why did you pinch my smurf?
To see if you were a real Smurf! A fake one wouldn't have shouted!
Go quickly and smurf the others!
A fake Smurf! Incredible!
Hey! Smu-urf!
Yes?
Turn around!
Why?
You'll see why! Let's go!
?
OWW!
You're okay!
POW
But I just wanted to see if you were a real Smurf!
?
Ha! Ha! Ha! I'll be avenged tonight!
What's going on?
OWW!
OWW!
Oww!
Oww!
Oww!
What...? Are they crazy?

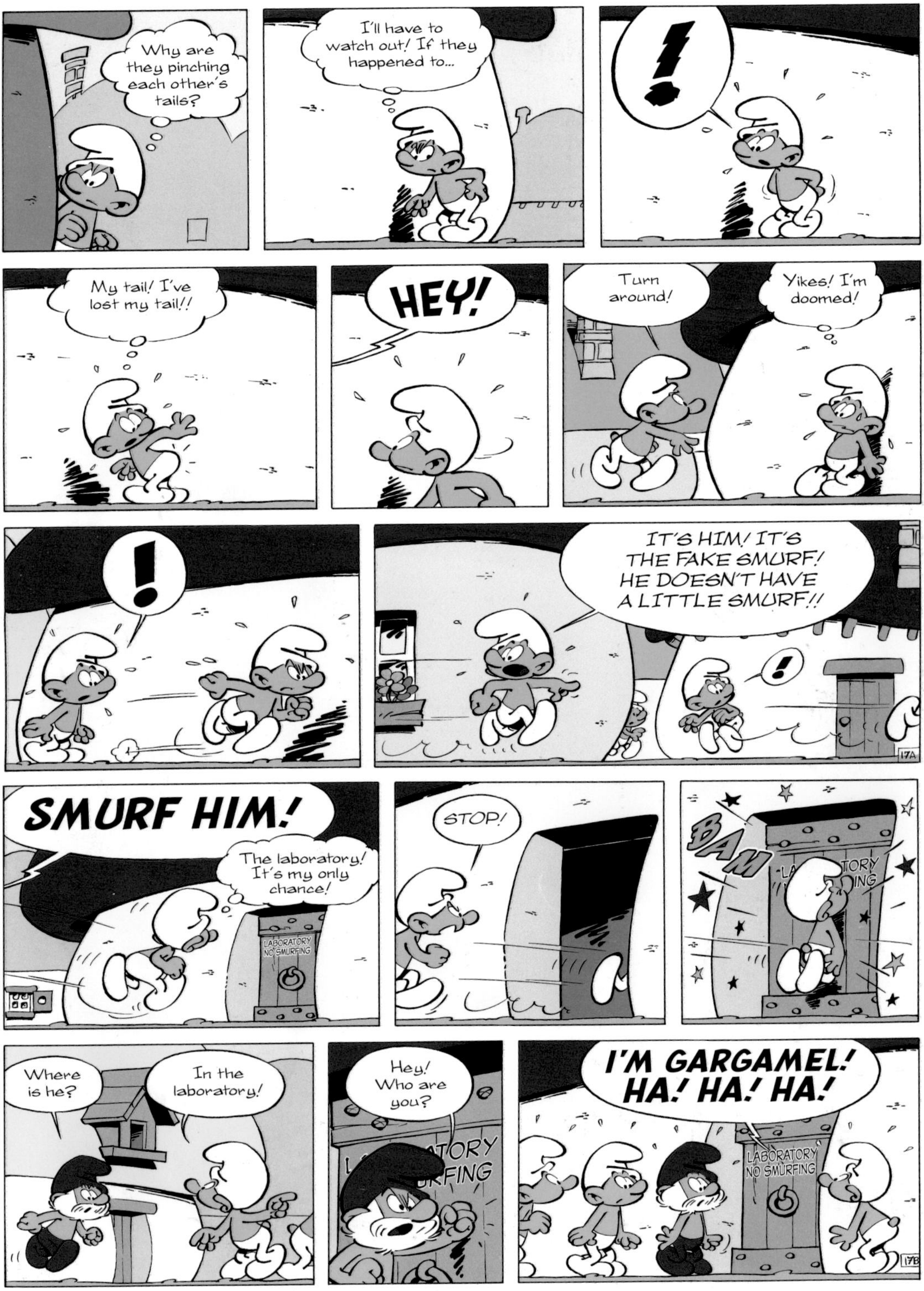

Why are they pinching each other's tails?
I'll have to watch out! If they happened to...
!
My tail! I've lost my tail!!
HEY!
Turn around!
Yikes! I'm doomed!
!
IT'S HIM! IT'S THE FAKE SMURF! HE DOESN'T HAVE A LITTLE SMURF!!
!
17A
SMURF HIM!
The laboratory! It's my only chance!
LABORATORY NO SMURFING
STOP!
BAM
Where is he?
In the laboratory!
Hey! Who are you?
I'M GARGAMEL! HA! HA! HA!
LABORATORY NO SMURFING
17B

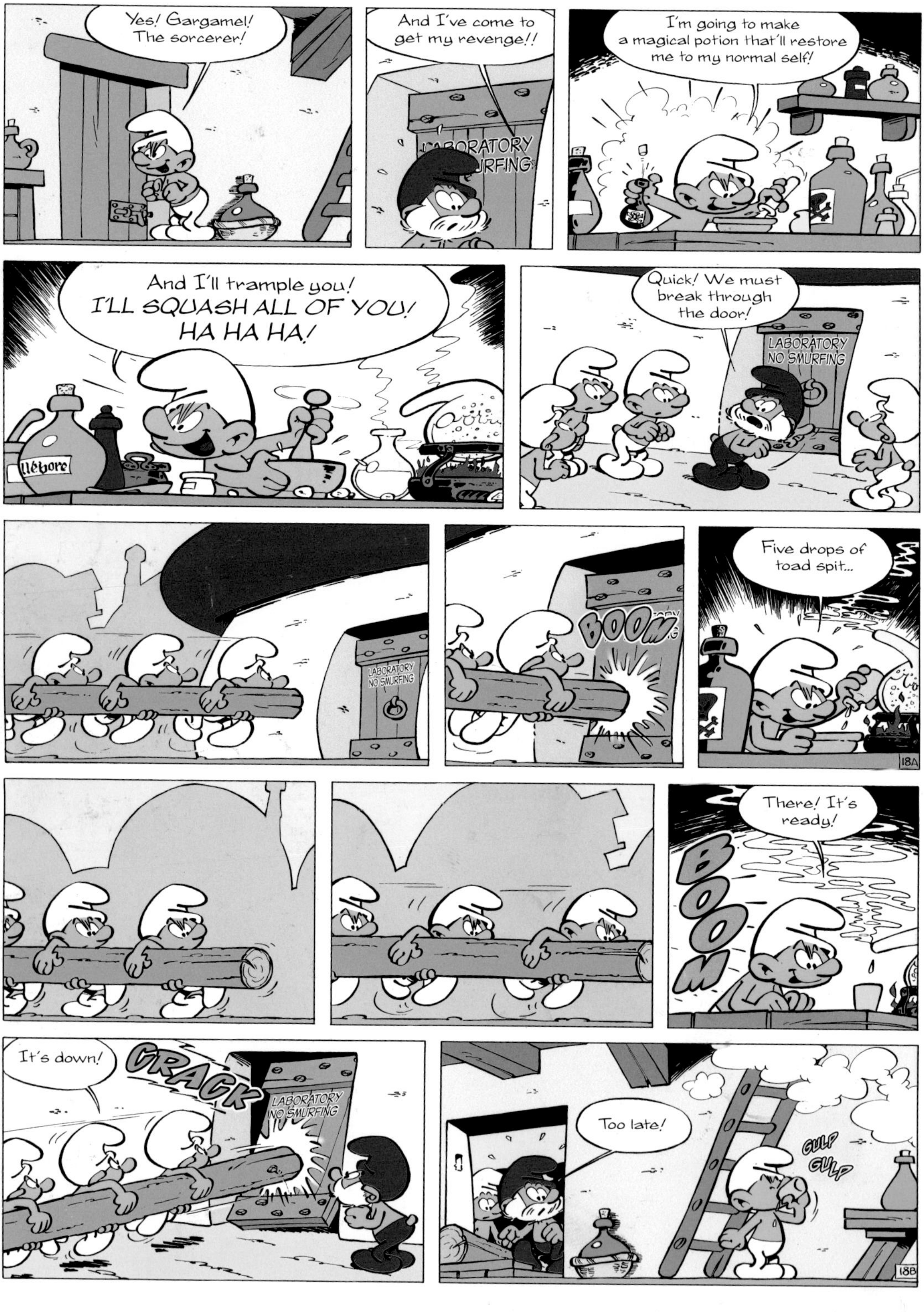

Yes! Gargamel! The sorcerer!
And I've come to get my revenge!!
I'm going to make a magical potion that'll restore me to my normal self!
And I'll trample you! I'LL SQUASH ALL OF YOU! HA HA HA!
Quick! We must break through the door!
LABORATORY NO SMURFING
LABORATORY NO SMURFING
BOOM
Five drops of toad spit...
18A
There! It's ready!
BOOM
It's down!
CRACK
LABORATORY NO SMURFING
Too late!
GULP GULP
18B

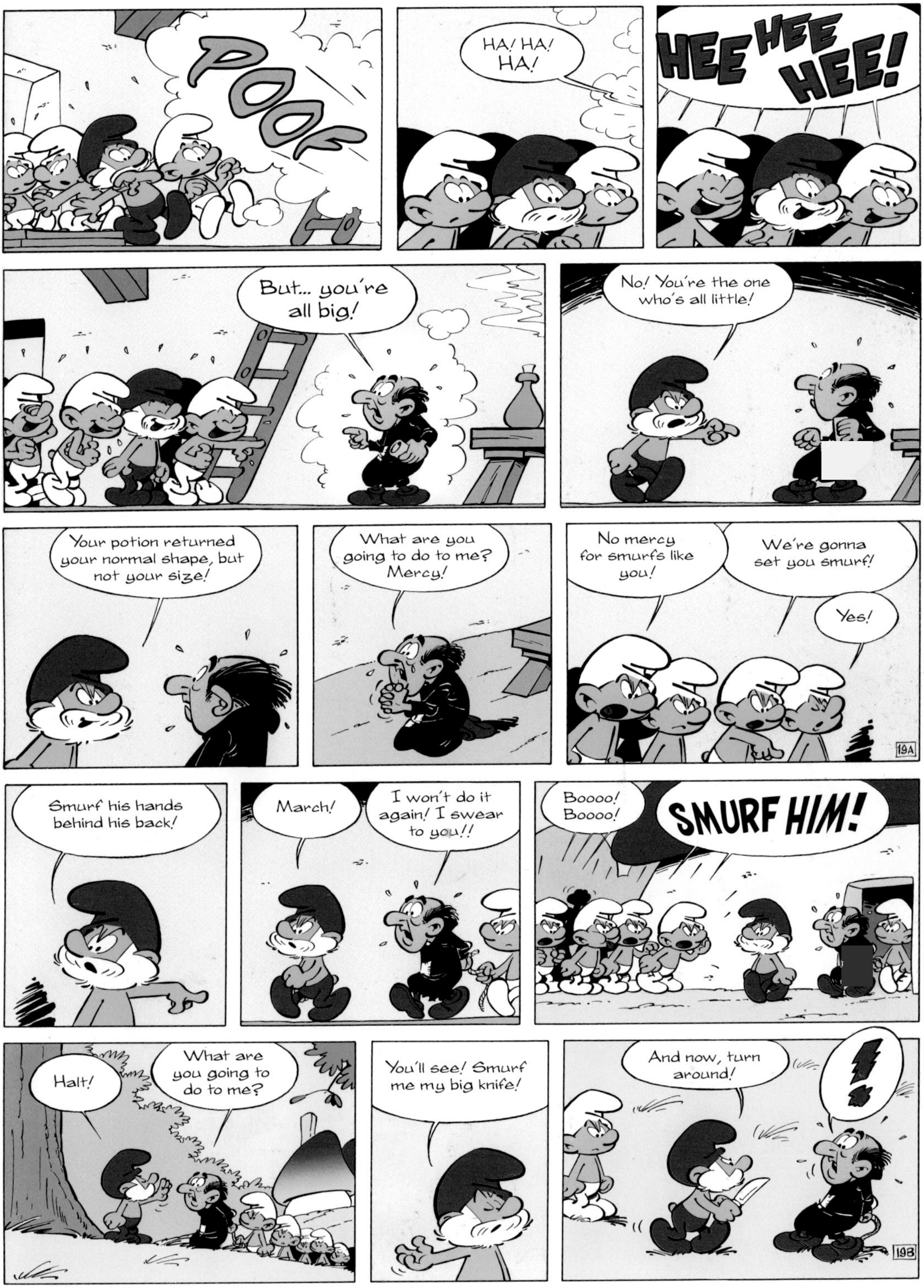
POOF
HA! HA! HA!
HEE HEE HEE!
But... you're all big!
No! You're the one who's all little!
Your potion returned your normal shape, but not your size!
What are you going to do to me? Mercy!
No mercy for smurfs like you!
We're gonna set you smurf!
Yes!
19A
Smurf his hands behind his back!
March!
I won't do it again! I swear to you!!
Boooo! Boooo!
SMURF HIM!
Halt!
What are you going to do to me?
You'll see! Smurf me my big knife!
And now, turn around!
19B

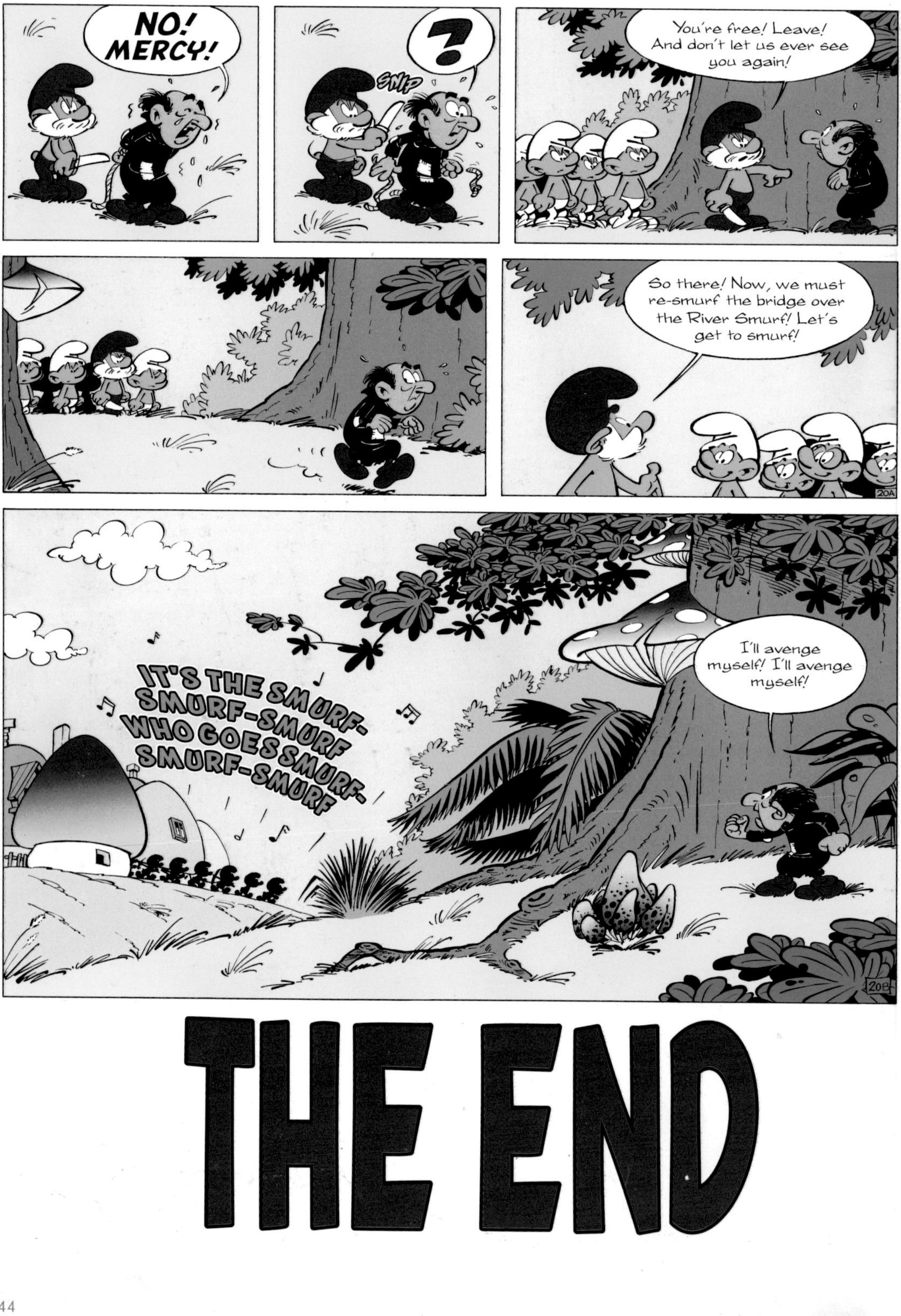
NO! MERCY!
?
SNIP
You're free! Leave! And don't let us ever see you again!
So there! Now, we must re-smurf the bridge over the River Smurf! Let's get to smurf!
20A
IT'S THE SMURF-SMURF WHO GOES SMURF-SMURF-SMURF
I'll avenge myself! I'll avenge myself!
20B

THE END

THE HUNDREDTH SMURF

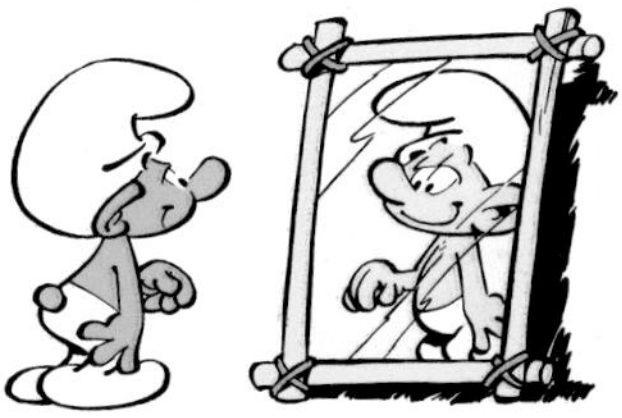

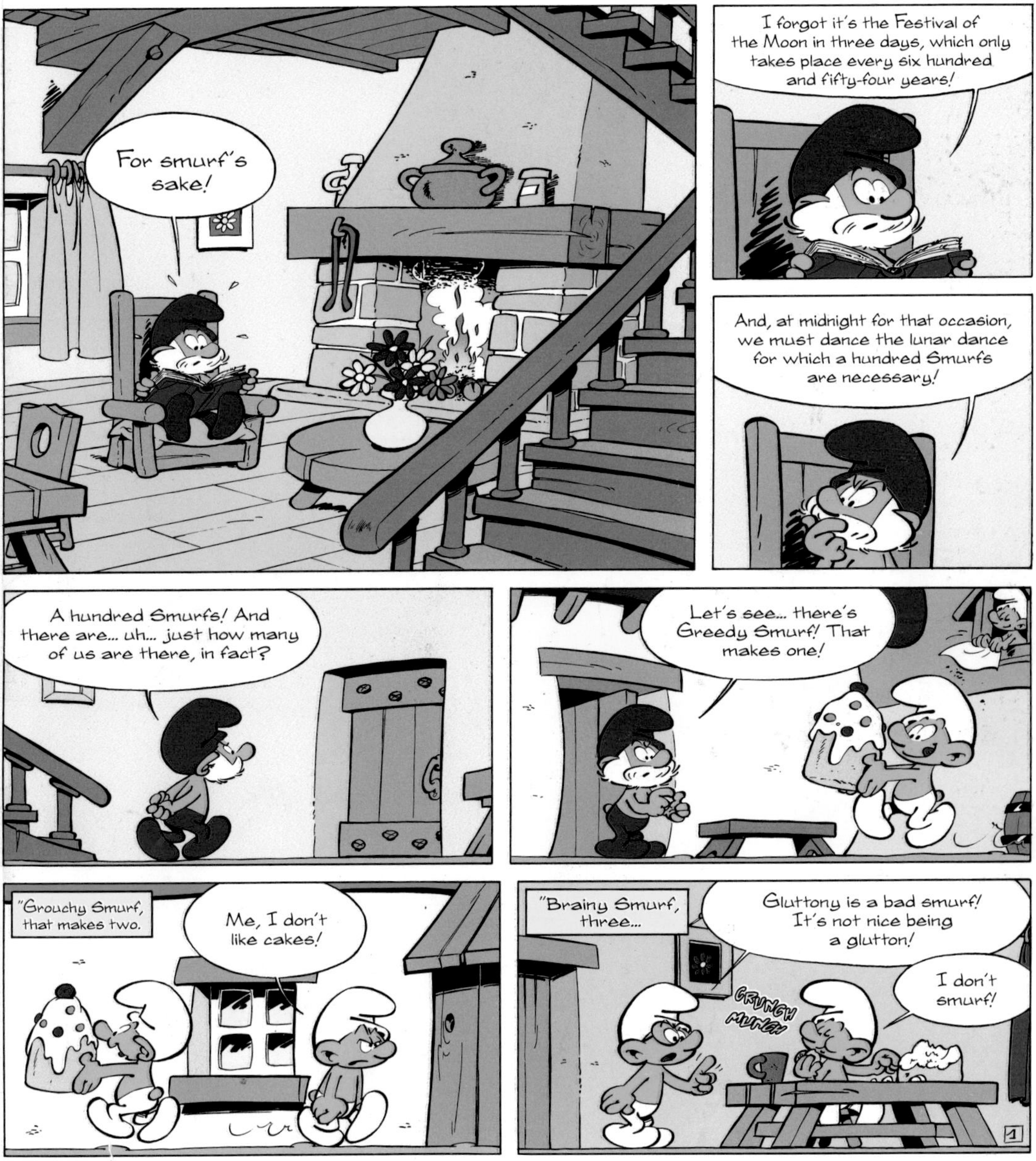

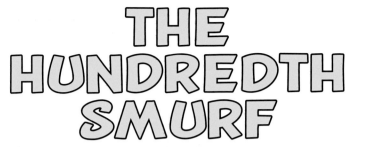

For smurf's sake!
I forgot it's the Festival of the Moon in three days, which only takes place every six hundred and fifty-four years!
And, at midnight for that occasion, we must dance the lunar dance for which a hundred Smurfs are necessary!
A hundred Smurfs! And there are... uh... just how many of us are there, in fact?
Let's see... there's Greedy Smurf! That makes one!
"Grouchy Smurf, that makes two.
Me, I don't like cakes!
"Brainy Smurf, three...
Gluttony is a bad smurf! It's not nice being a glutton!
CRUNCH MUNCH
I don't smurf!
1

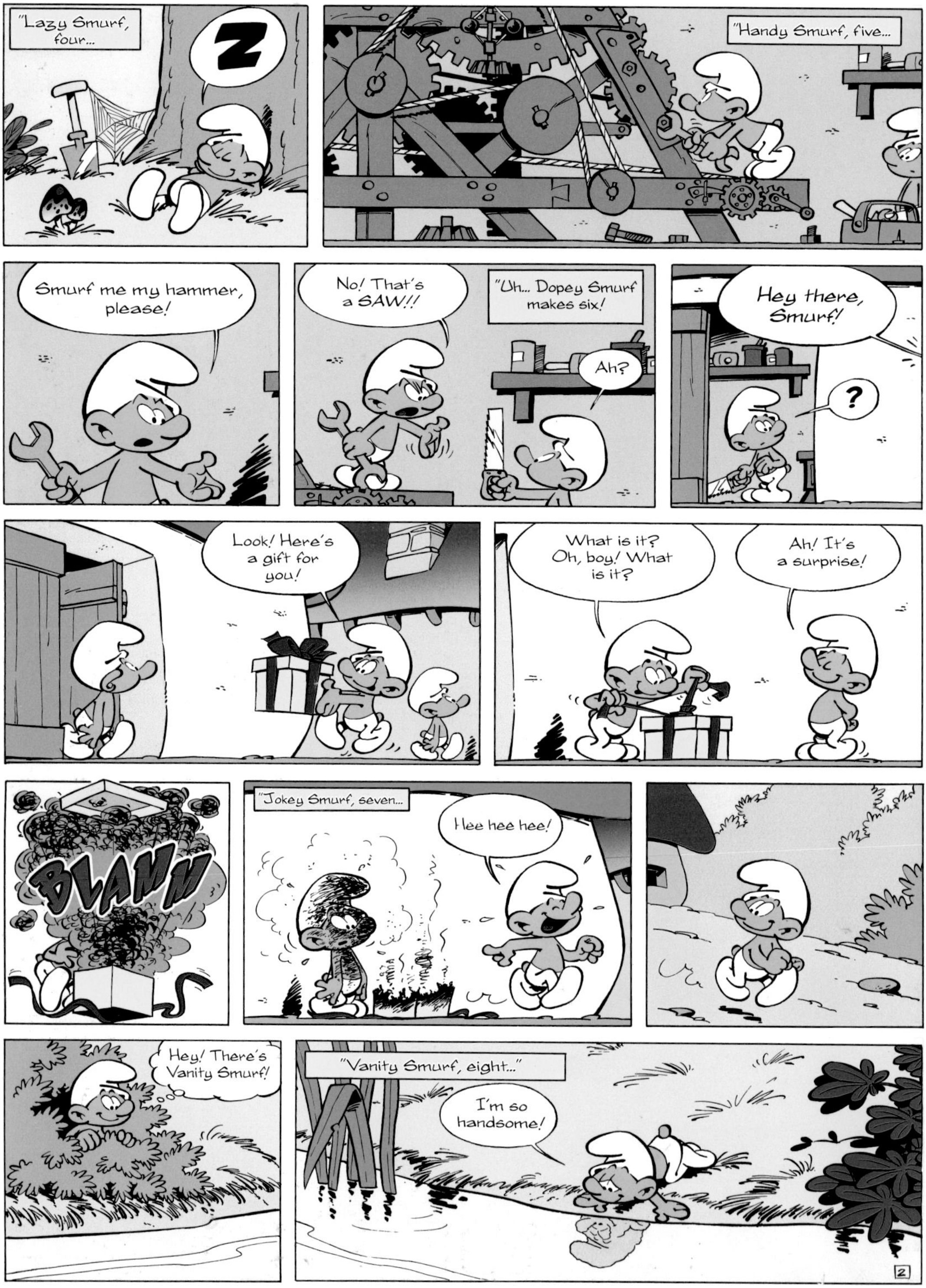

"Lazy Smurf, four...
Z
"Handy Smurf, five...
Smurf me my hammer, please!
No! That's a SAW!!
"Uh... Dopey Smurf makes six!
Ah?
Hey there, Smurf!
?
Look! Here's a gift for you!
What is it? Oh, boy! What is it?
Ah! It's a surprise!
BLAMM
"Jokey Smurf, seven...
Hee hee hee!
Hey! There's Vanity Smurf!
"Vanity Smurf, eight..."
I'm so handsome!
2

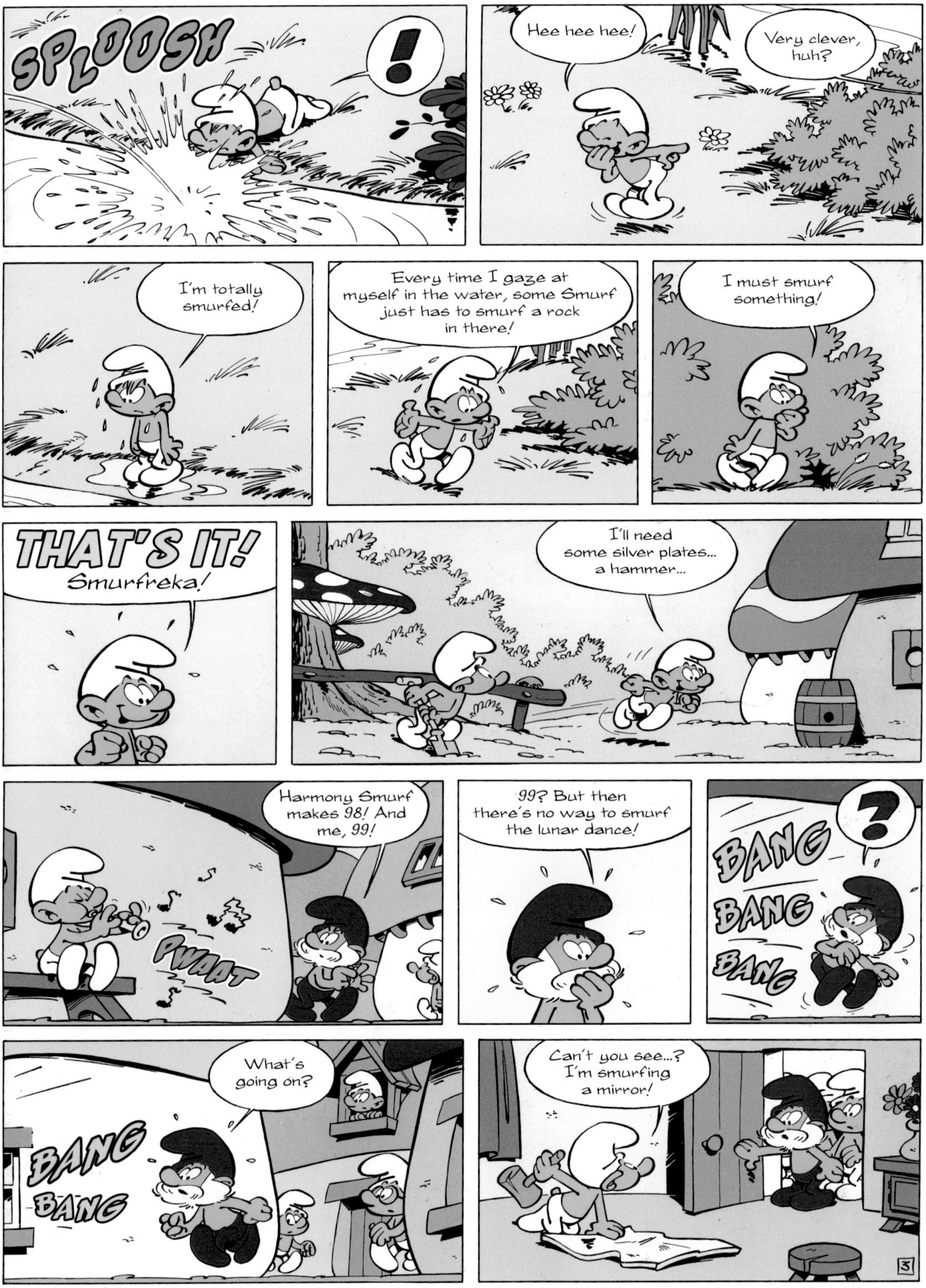

SPLOOSH
!
Hee hee hee!
Very clever, huh?
I'm totally smurfed!
Every time I gaze at myself in the water, some Smurf just has to smurf a rock in there!
I must smurf something!
THAT'S IT! Smurfreka!
I'll need some silver plates... a hammer...
Harmony Smurf makes 98! And me, 99!
PWAAT
99? But then there's no way to smurf the lunar dance!
?
BANG
BANG
BANG
What's going on?
BANG
BANG
Can't you see...? I'm smurfing a mirror!
3

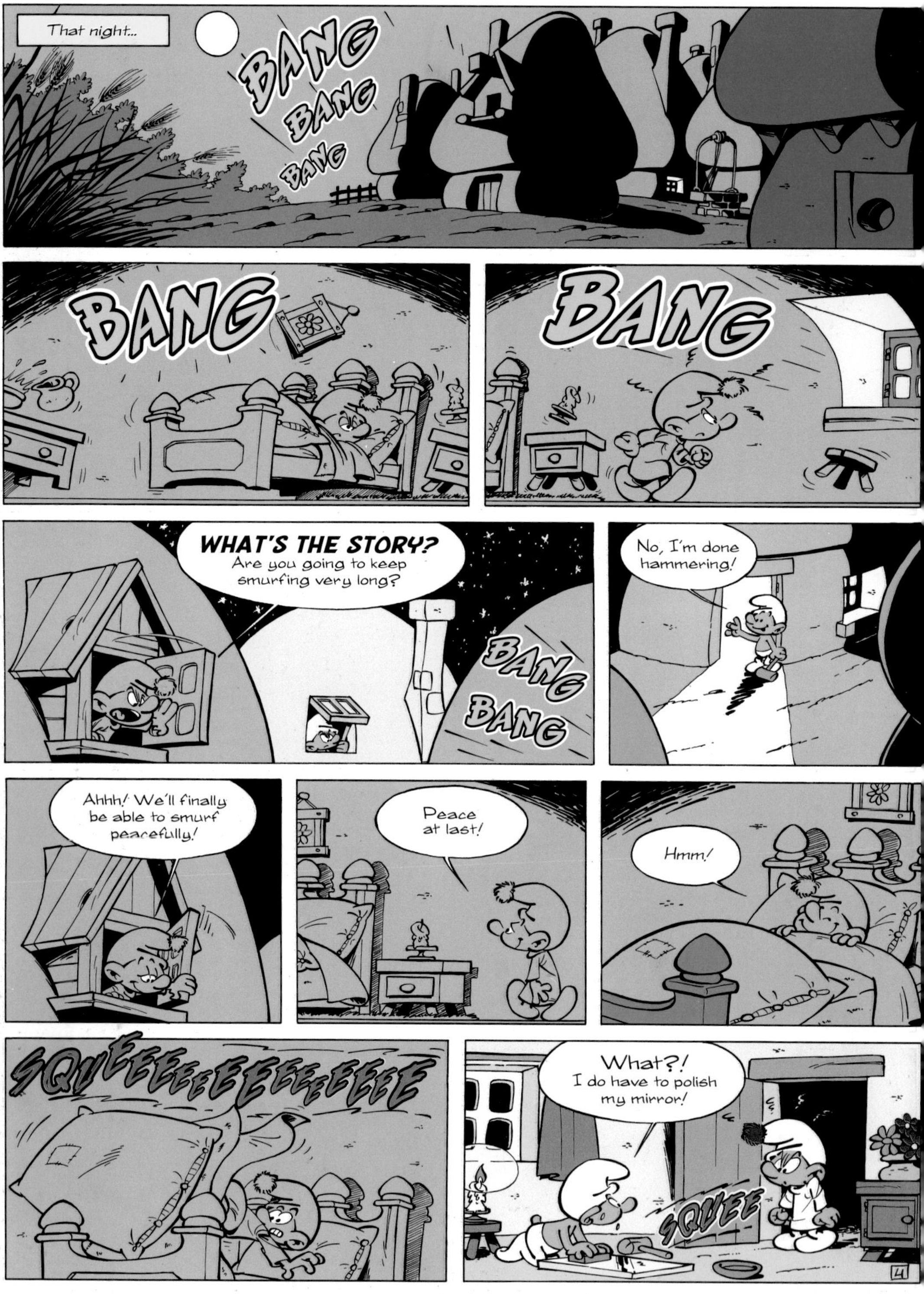
That night...
BANG
BANG
BANG
BANG
BANG
WHAT'S THE STORY?
Are you going to keep smurfing very long?
BANG
BANG
No, I'm done hammering!
Ahhh! We'll finally be able to smurf peacefully!
Peace at last!
Hmm!
SQUEEEEEEEEEEEEEE
What?!
I do have to polish my mirror!
SQUEE
4

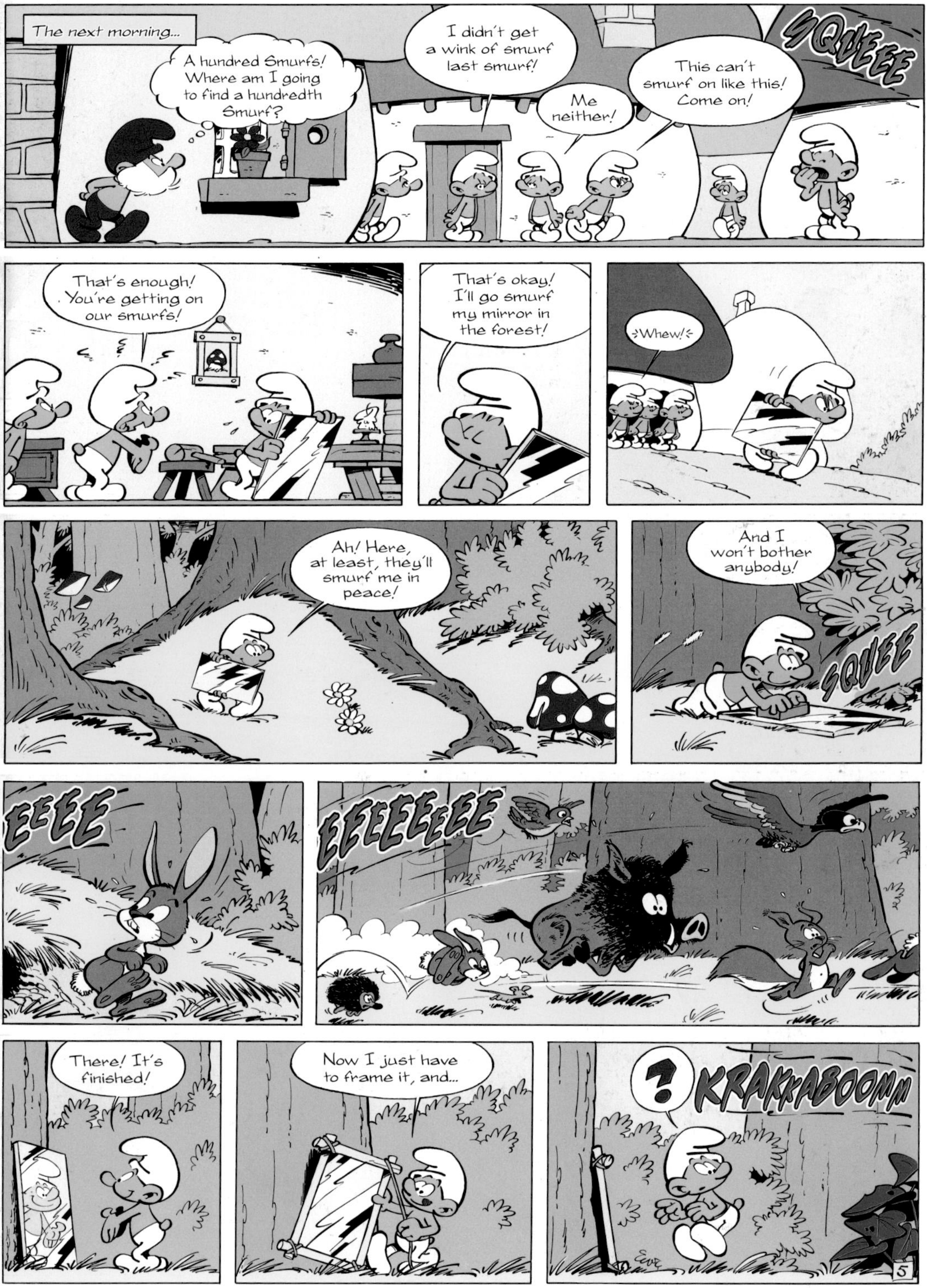

The next morning...
A hundred Smurfs! Where am I going to find a hundredth Smurf?
I didn't get a wink of smurf last smurf!
Me neither!
This can't smurf on like this! Come on!
SQUEEE
That's enough! You're getting on our smurfs!
That's okay! I'll go smurf my mirror in the forest!
Whew!
Ah! Here, at least, they'll smurf me in peace!
And I won't bother anybody!
SQUEE
EEEE
EEEEEEEEE
There! It's finished!
Now I just have to frame it, and...
?
KRAKKABOOMM
5

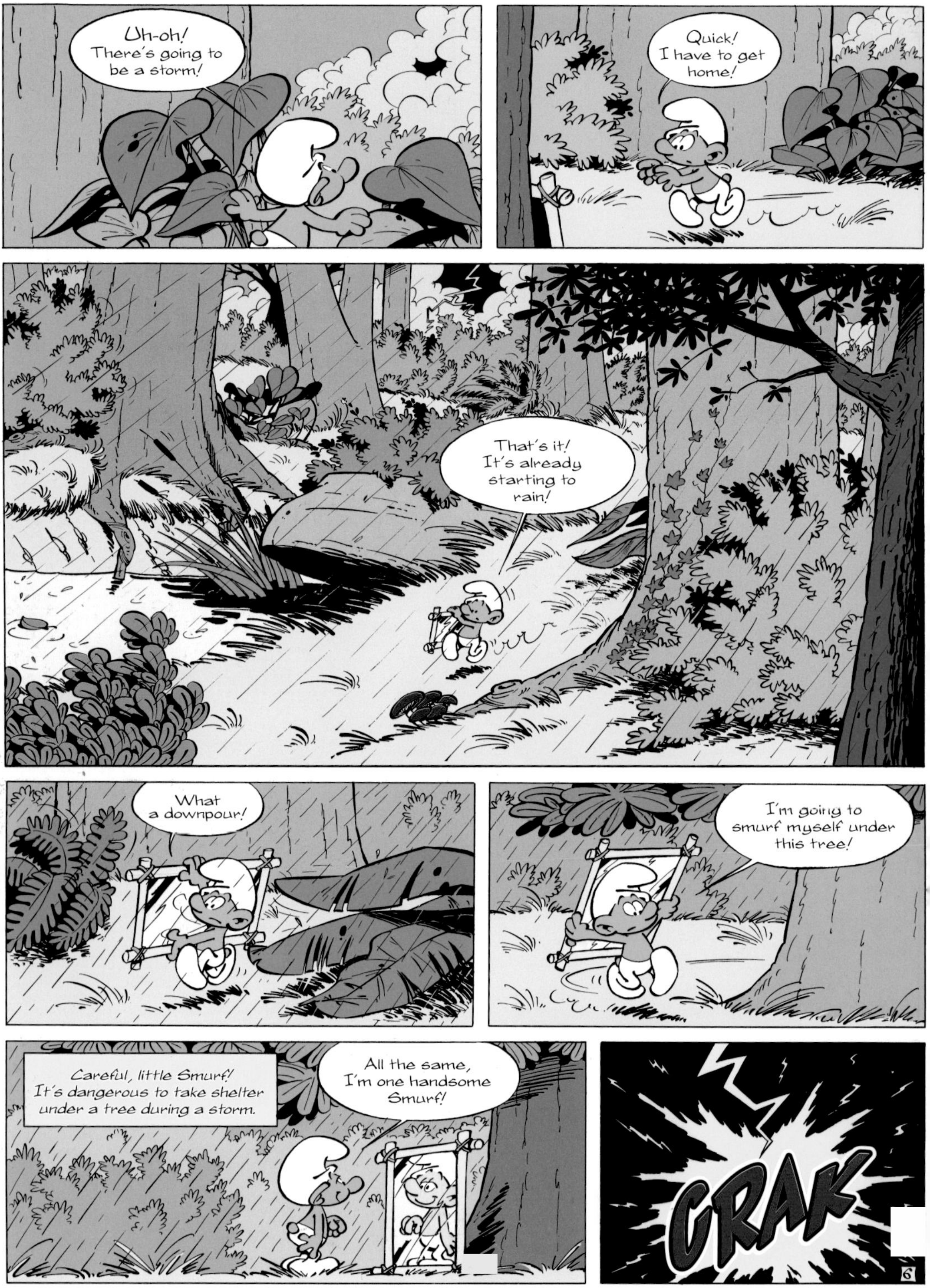

Uh-oh! There's going to be a storm!
Quick! I have to get home!
That's it! It's already starting to rain!
What a downpour!
I'm going to smurf myself under this tree!
Careful, little Smurf! It's dangerous to take shelter under a tree during a storm.
All the same, I'm one handsome Smurf!
CRAK
6

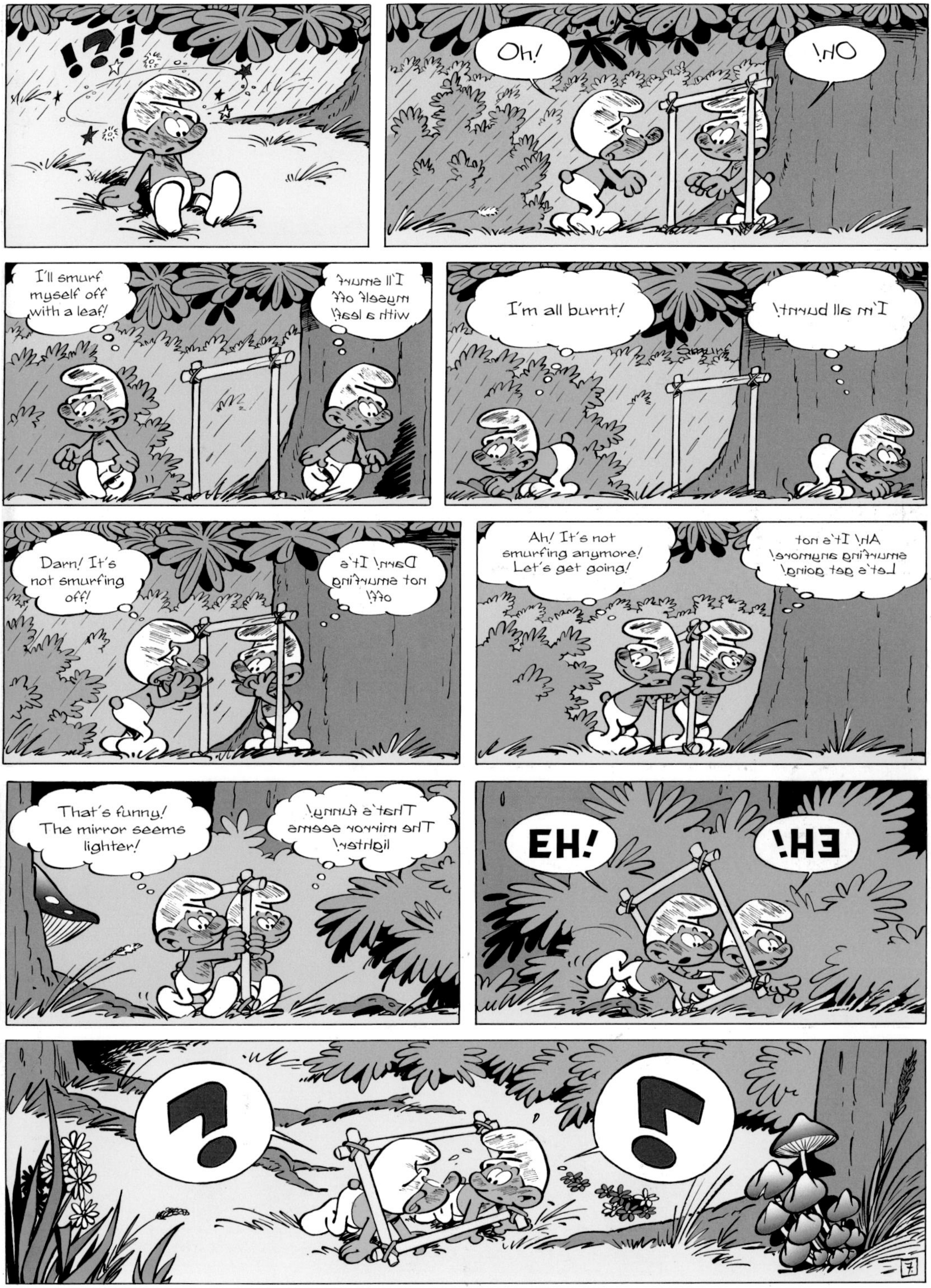
!?!
Oh!
Oh!
I'll smurf myself off with a leaf!
I'll smurf myself off with a leaf!
I'm all burnt!
I'm all burnt!
Darn! It's not smurfing off!
Darn! It's not smurfing off!
Ah! It's not smurfing anymore! Let's get going!
Ah! It's not smurfing anymore! Let's get going!
That's funny! The mirror seems lighter!
That's funny! The mirror seems lighter!
EH!
EH!
7

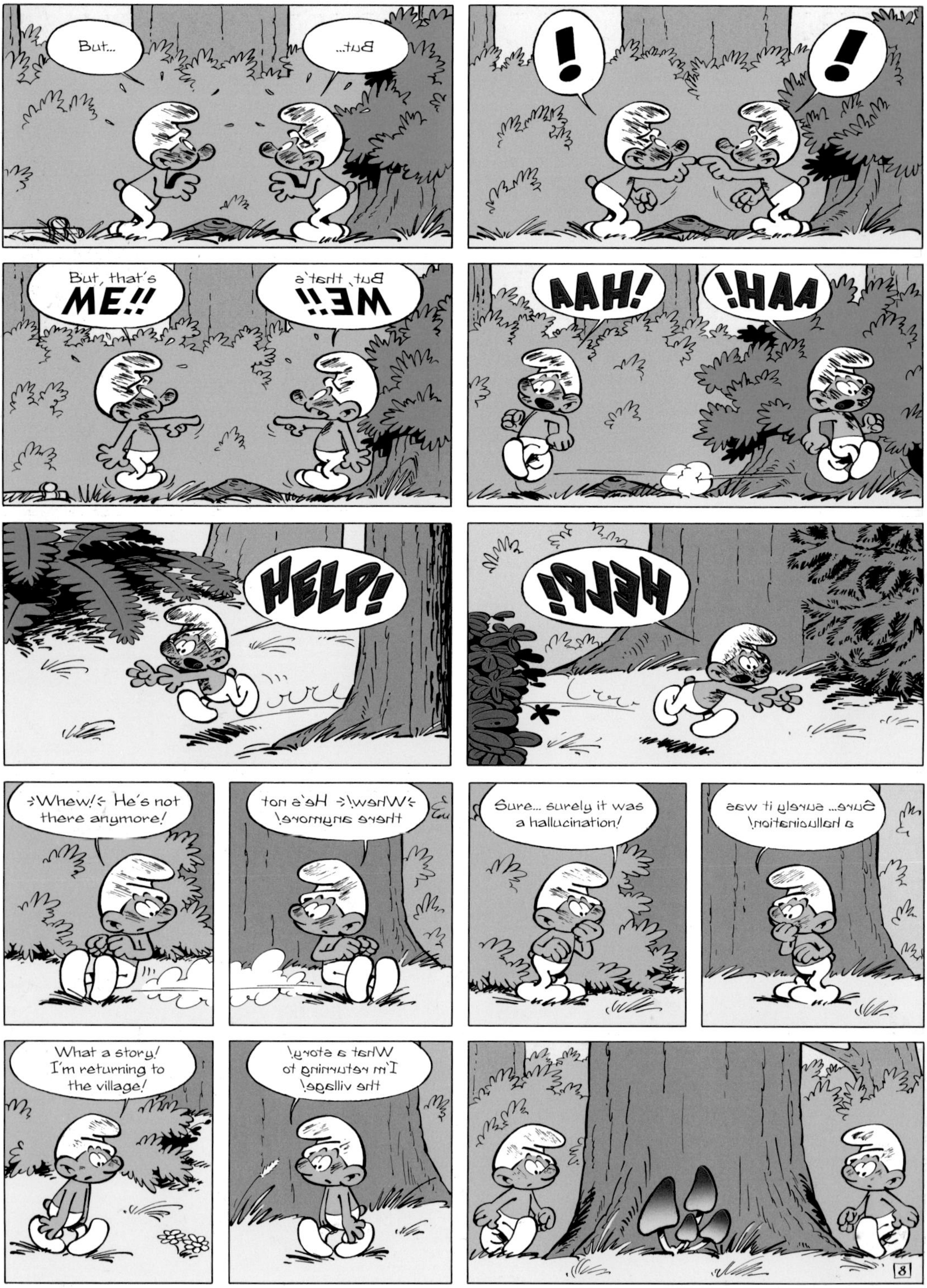

But...
But...
!
!
But, that's ME!!
But, that's ME!!
AAH!
AAH!
HELP!
HELP!
Whew! He's not there anymore!
Whew! He's not there anymore!
Sure... surely it was a hallucination!
Sure... surely it was a hallucination!
What a story! I'm returning to the village!
What a story! I'm returning to the village!
8

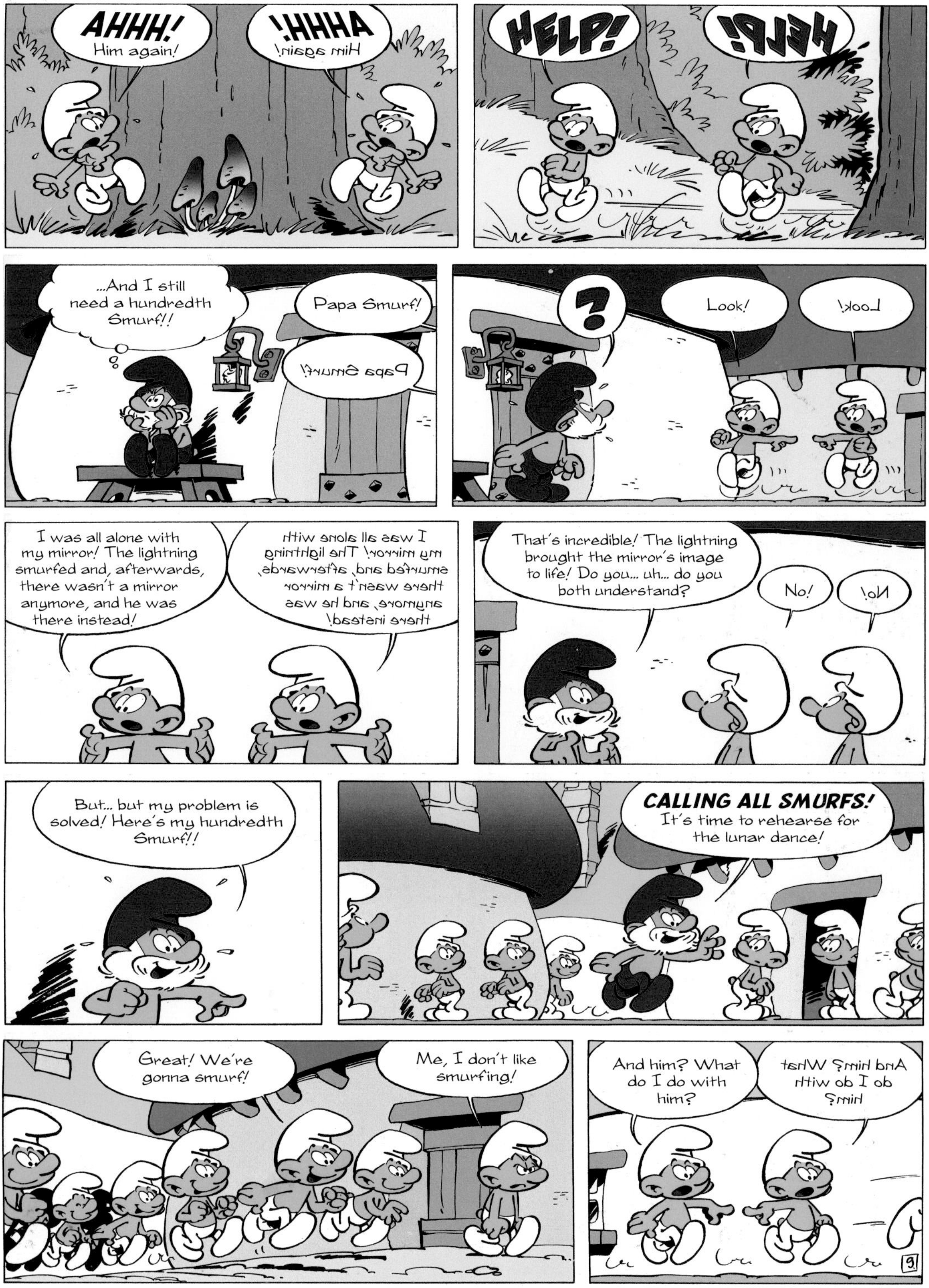
AHHH! Him again!
AHHH! Him again!
HELP!
HELP!
...And I still need a hundredth Smurf!!
Papa Smurf!
Papa Smurf!
?
Look!
Look!
I was all alone with my mirror! The lightning smurfed and, afterwards, there wasn't a mirror anymore, and he was there instead!
I was all alone with my mirror! The lightning smurfed and, afterwards, there wasn't a mirror anymore, and he was there instead!
That's incredible! The lightning brought the mirror's image to life! Do you... uh... do you both understand?
No!
No!
But... but my problem is solved! Here's my hundredth Smurf!!
CALLING ALL SMURFS! It's time to rehearse for the lunar dance!
Great! We're gonna smurf!
Me, I don't like smurfing!
And him? What do I do with him?
And him? What do I do with him?
9

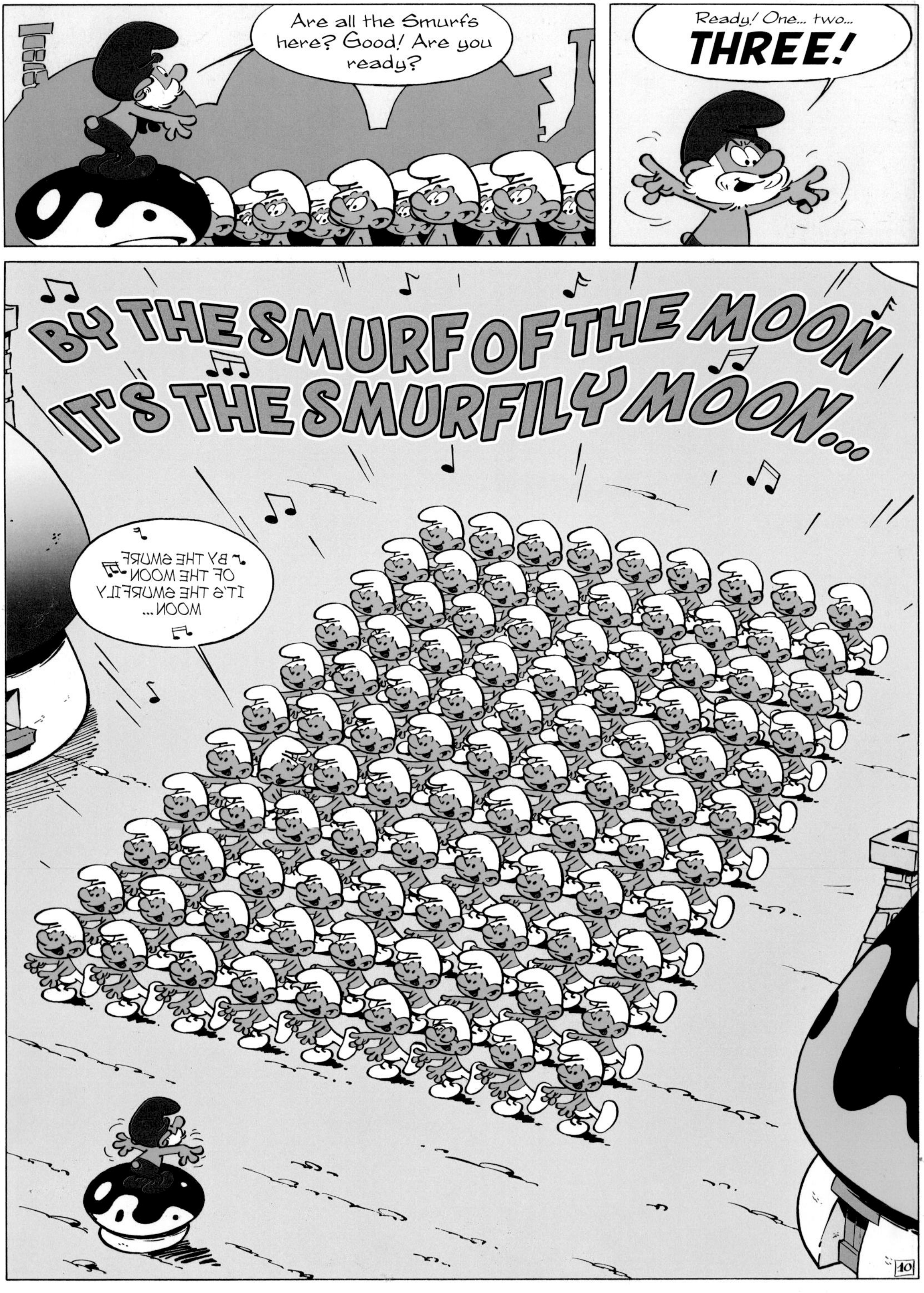
Are all the Smurfs here? Good! Are you ready?
Ready! One... two...
THREE!
BY THE SMURF OF THE MOON IT'S THE SMURFILY MOON...
BY THE SMURF OF THE MOON IT'S THE SMURFILY MOON...

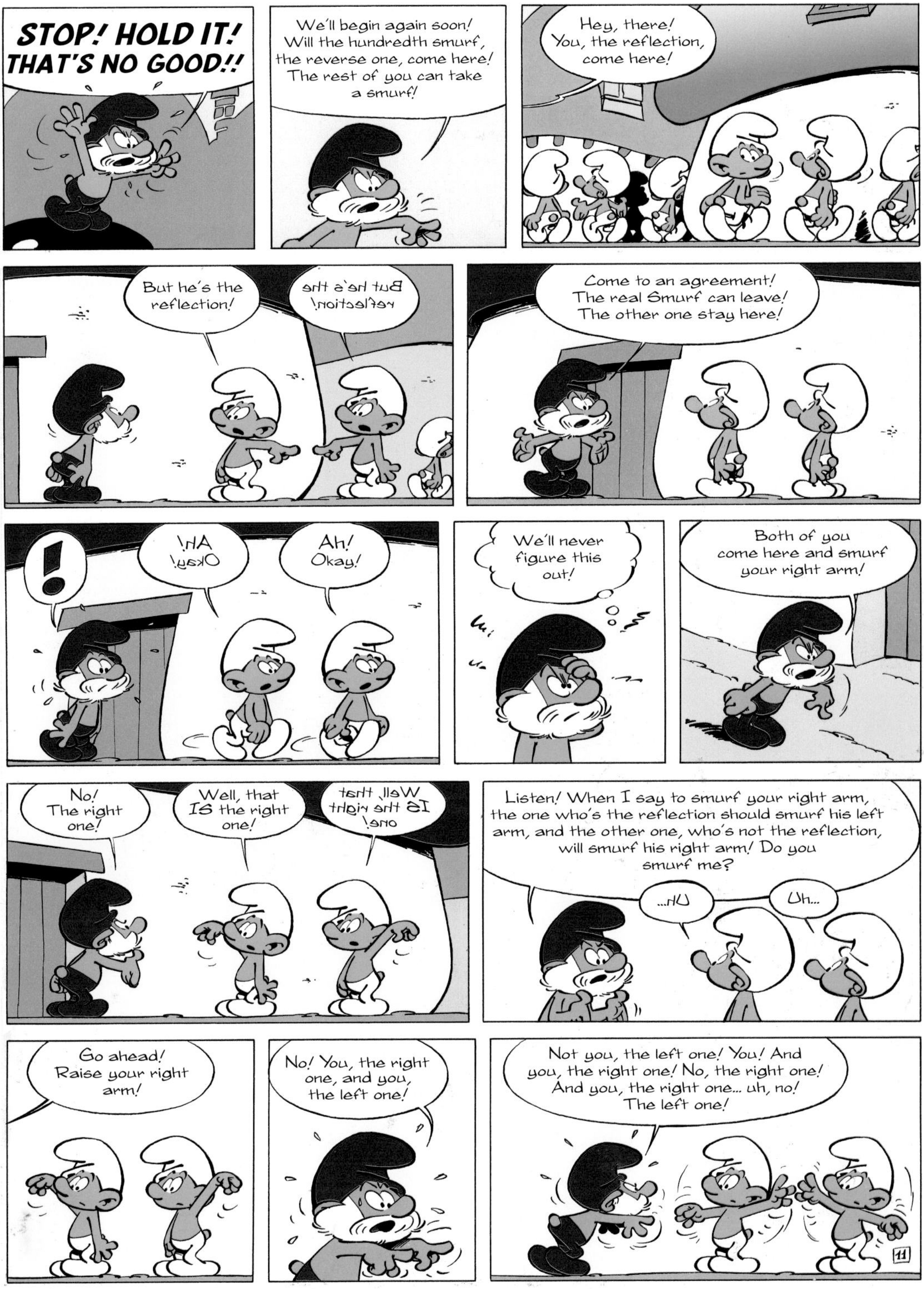
STOP! HOLD IT! THAT'S NO GOOD!!
We'll begin again soon! Will the hundredth smurf, the reverse one, come here! The rest of you can take a smurf!
Hey, there! You, the reflection, come here!
But he's the reflection!
But he's the reflection!
Come to an agreement! The real Smurf can leave! The other one stay here!
!
Ah! Okay!
Ah! Okay!
We'll never figure this out!
Both of you come here and smurf your right arm!
No! The right one!
Well, that IS the right one!
Well, that IS the right one!
Listen! When I say to smurf your right arm, the one who's the reflection should smurf his left arm, and the other one, who's not the reflection, will smurf his right arm! Do you smurf me?
Uh...
Uh...
Go ahead! Raise your right arm!
No! You, the right one, and you, the left one!
Not you, the left one! You! And you, the right one! No, the right one! And you, the right one... uh, no! The left one!
11

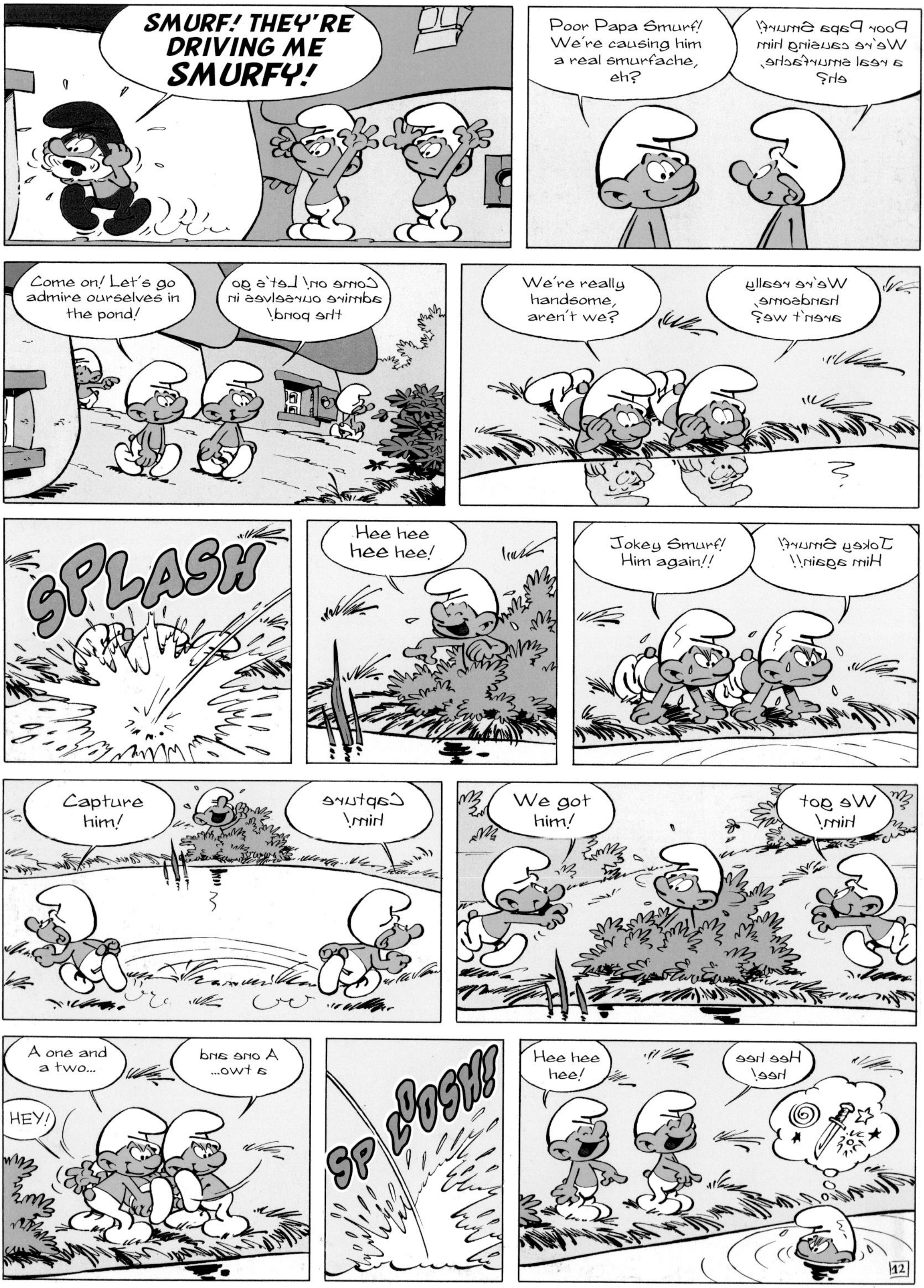

SMURF! THEY'RE DRIVING ME SMURFY!
Poor Papa Smurf! We're causing him a real smurfache, eh?
Poor Papa Smurf! We're causing him a real smurfache, eh?
Come on! Let's go admire ourselves in the pond!
Come on! Let's go admire ourselves in the pond!
We're really handsome, aren't we?
We're really handsome, aren't we?
SPLASH
Hee hee hee hee!
Jokey Smurf! Him again!!
Jokey Smurf! Him again!!
Capture him!
Capture him!
We got him!
We got him!
A one and a two...
A one and a two...
HEY!
SPLOOSH!
Hee hee hee!
Hee hee hee!
12

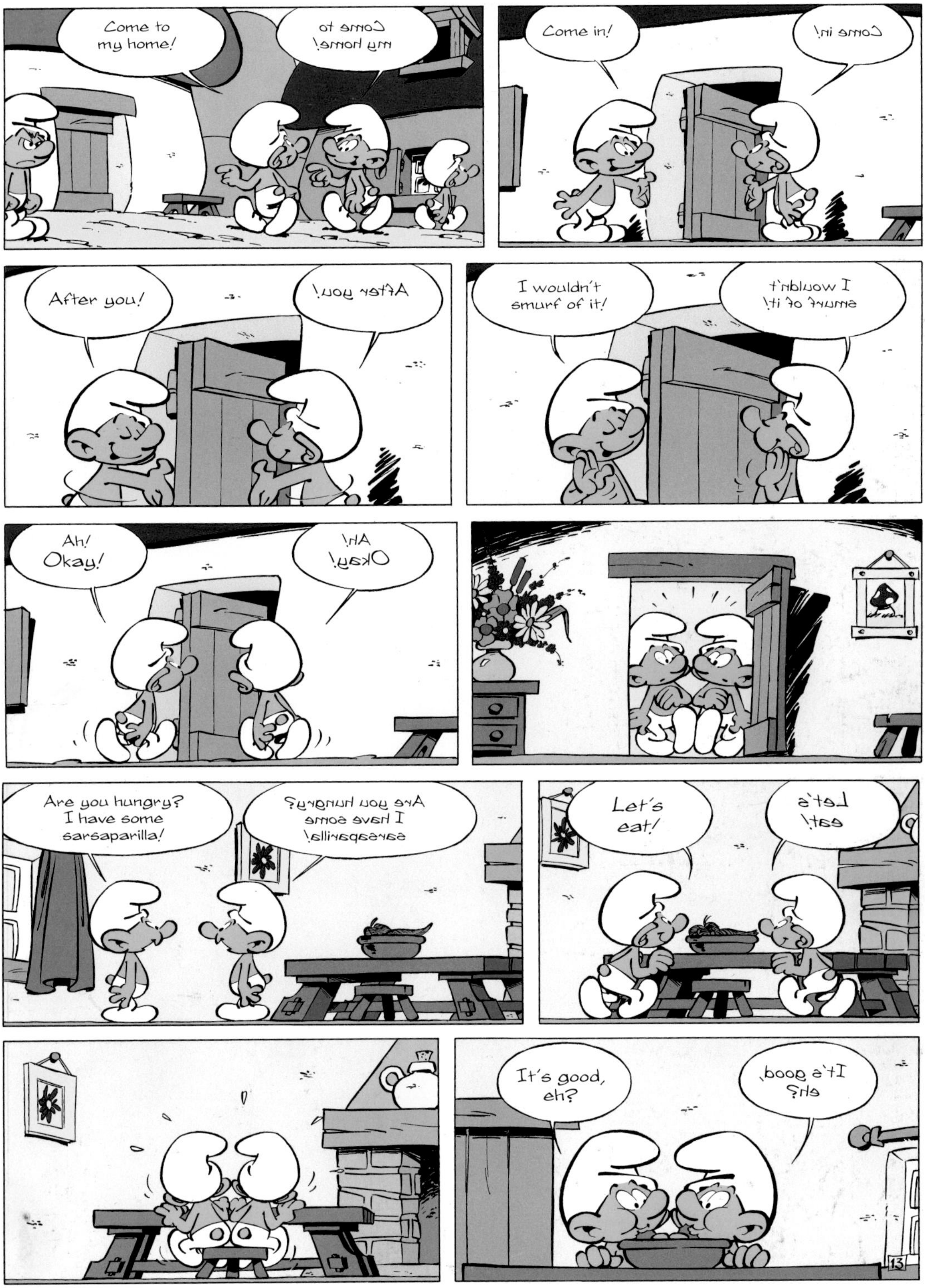
Come to my home!
Come to my home!
Come in!
Come in!
After you!
After you!
I wouldn't smurf of it!
I wouldn't smurf of it!
Ah! Okay!
Ah! Okay!
Are you hungry? I have some sarsaparilla!
Are you hungry? I have some sarsaparilla!
Let's eat!
Let's eat!
It's good, eh?
It's good, eh?

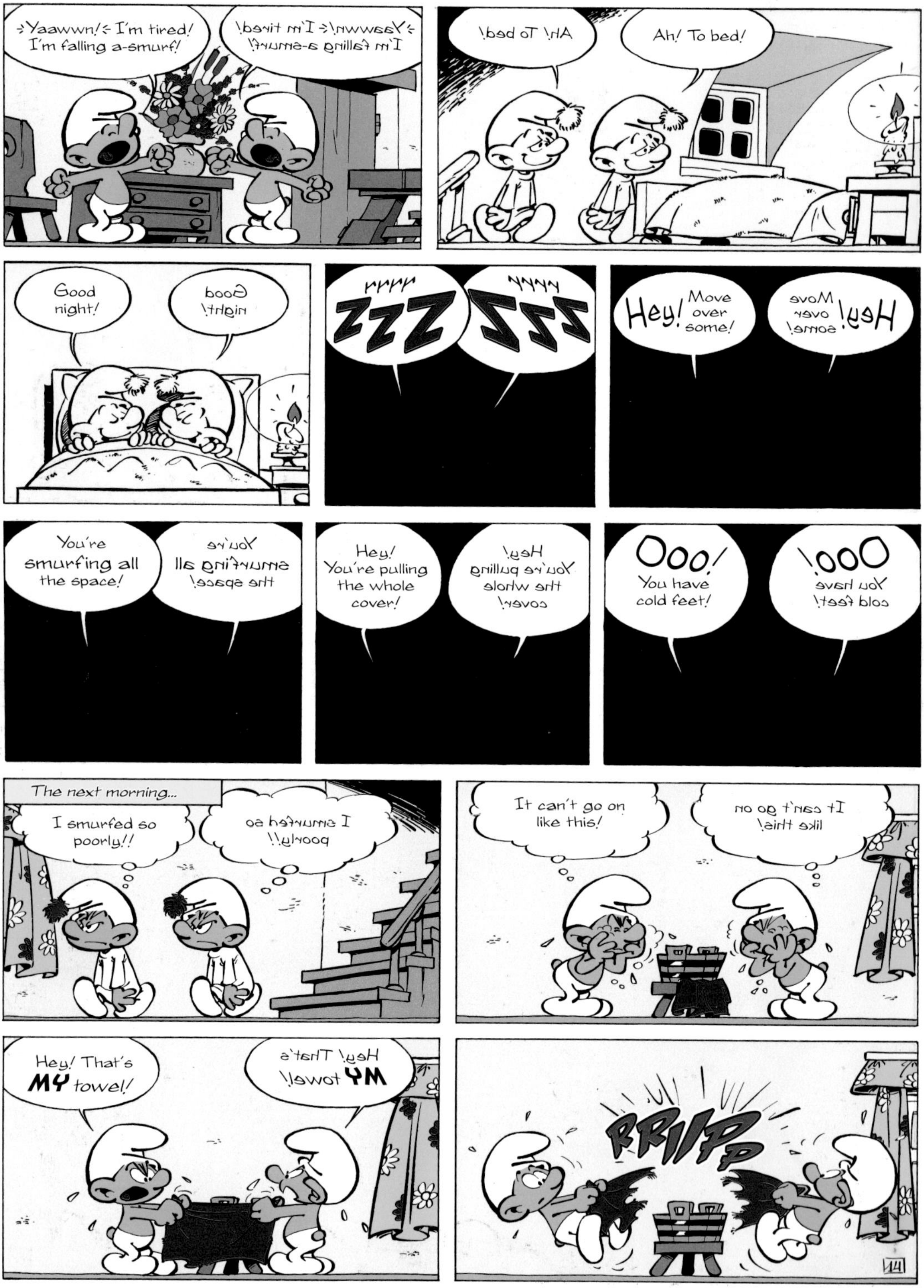
Yaawwn! I'm tired! I'm falling a-smurf!
Yaawwn! I'm tired! I'm falling a-smurf!
Ah! To bed!
Ah! To bed!
Good night!
Good night!
rrrrr ZZZ
rrrrr ZZZ
Hey! Move over some!
Hey! Move over some!
You're smurfing all the space!
You're smurfing all the space!
Hey! You're pulling the whole cover!
Hey! You're pulling the whole cover!
OOO! You have cold feet!
OOO! You have cold feet!
The next morning...
I smurfed so poorly!!
I smurfed so poorly!!
It can't go on like this!
It can't go on like this!
Hey! That's MY towel!
Hey! That's MY towel!
RRIIPP
14

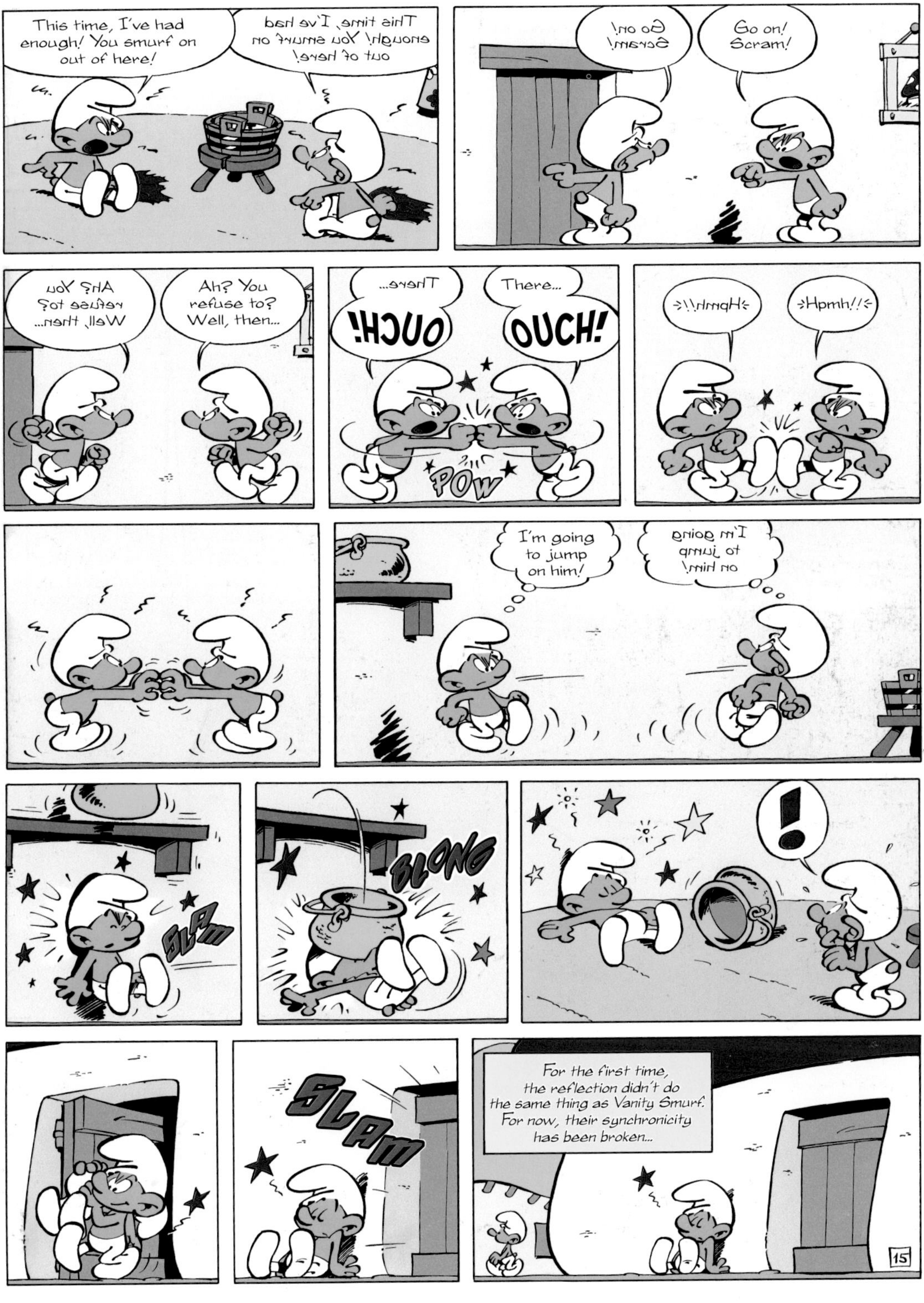

This time, I've had enough! You smurf on out of here!
This time, I've had enough! You smurf on out of here!
Go on! Scram!
Go on! Scram!
Ah? You refuse to? Well, then...
Ah? You refuse to? Well, then...
There...
OUCH!
There...
OUCH!
POW
Hpmh!!
Hpmh!!
I'm going to jump on him!
I'm going to jump on him!
SLAM
BLONG
!
SLAM
For the first time, the reflection didn't do the same thing as Vanity Smurf. For now, their synchronicity has been broken...
15

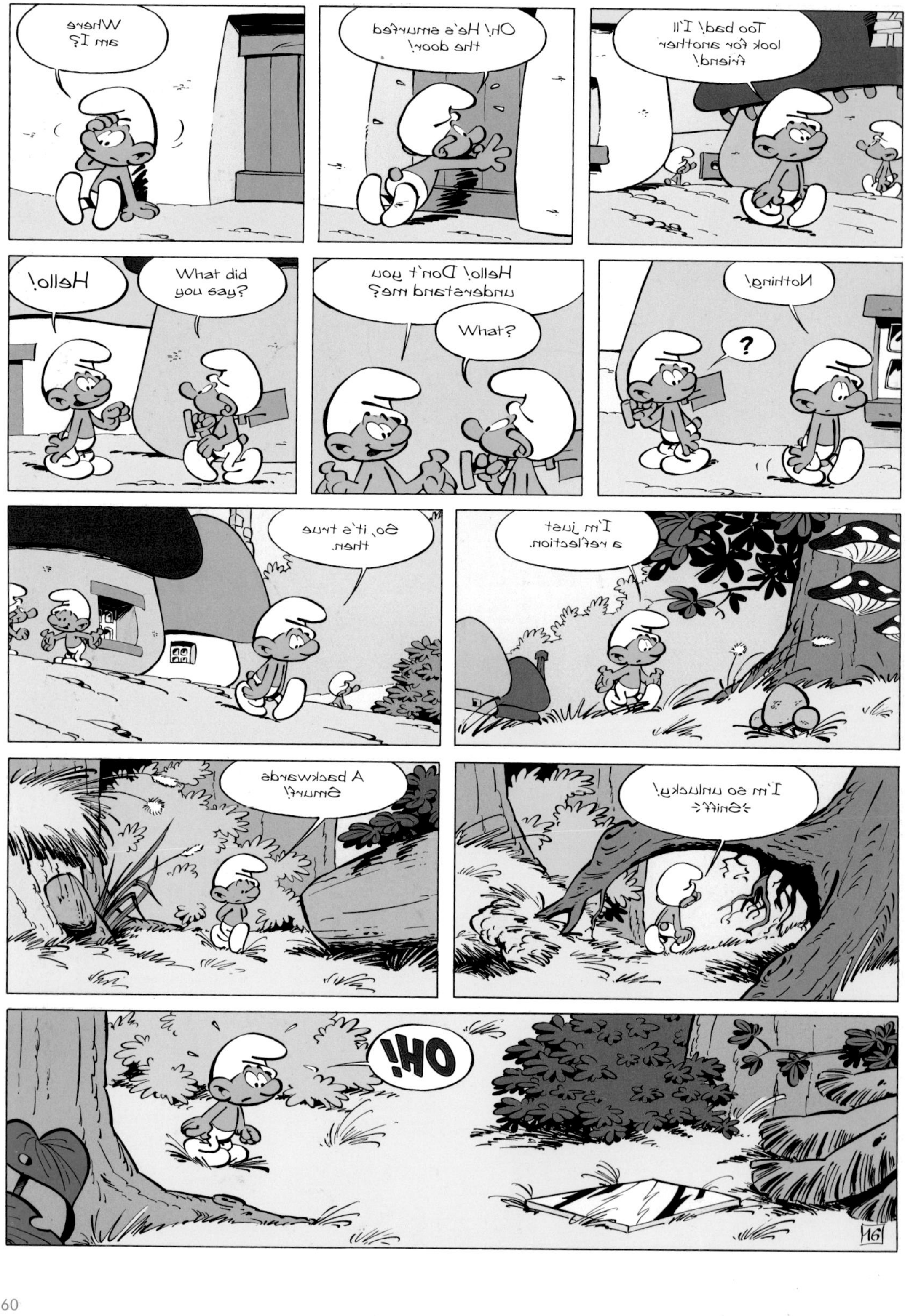

Where am I?
Oh! He's smurfed the door!
Too bad! I'll look for another friend!
Hello!
What did you say?
Hello! Don't you understand me?
What?
Nothing!
?
So, it's true then.
I'm just a reflection.
A backwards Smurf!
I'm so unlucky! *Sniff*
OH!
16

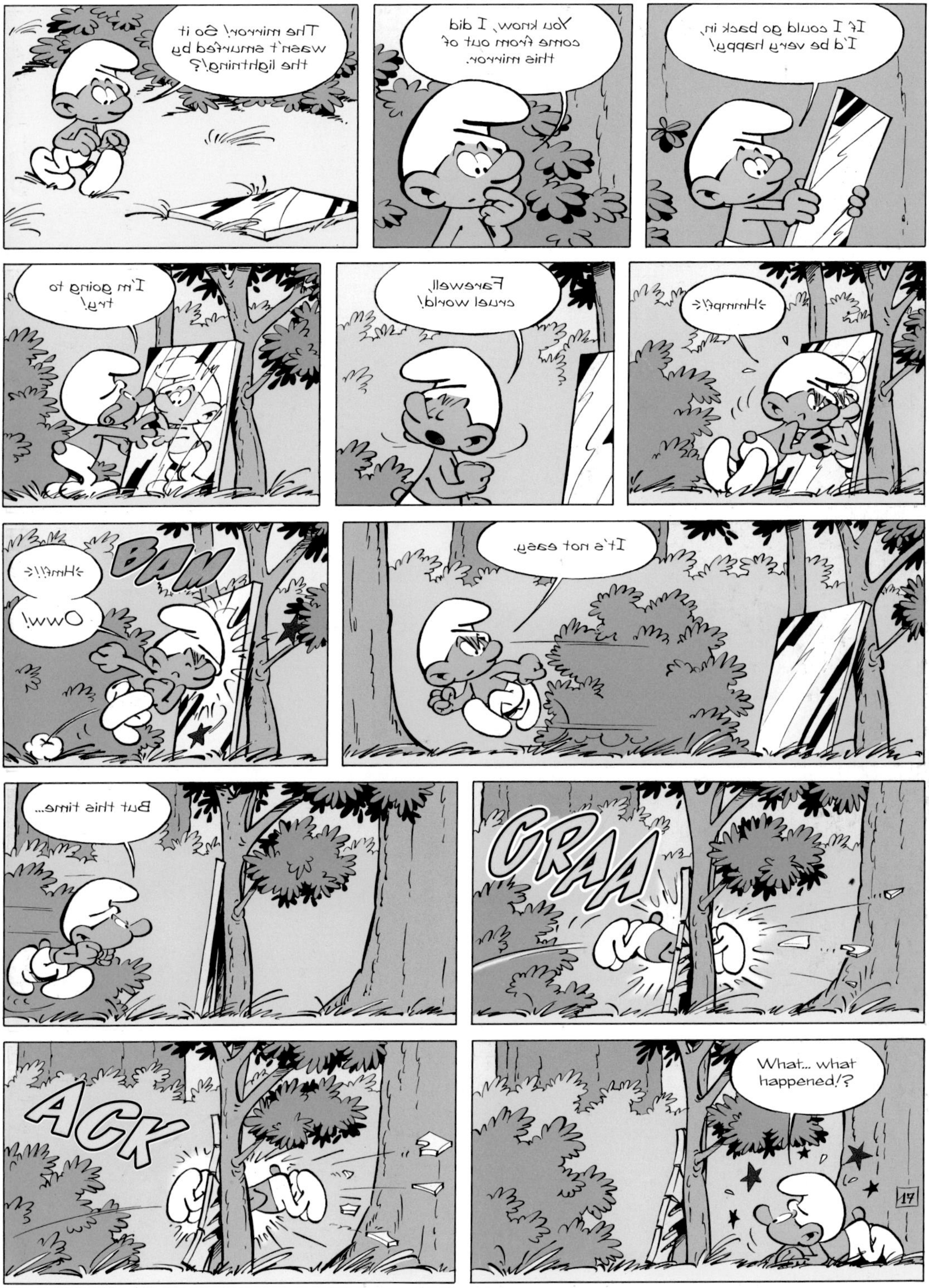

The mirror! So it wasn't smurfed by the lightning!?
You know, I did come from out of this mirror.
If I could go back in, I'd be very happy!
I'm going to try!
Farewell, cruel world!
Hmmpf!
BAM
Hmf!!
Oww!
It's not easy.
But this time...
CRAA
ACK
What... what happened!?
17

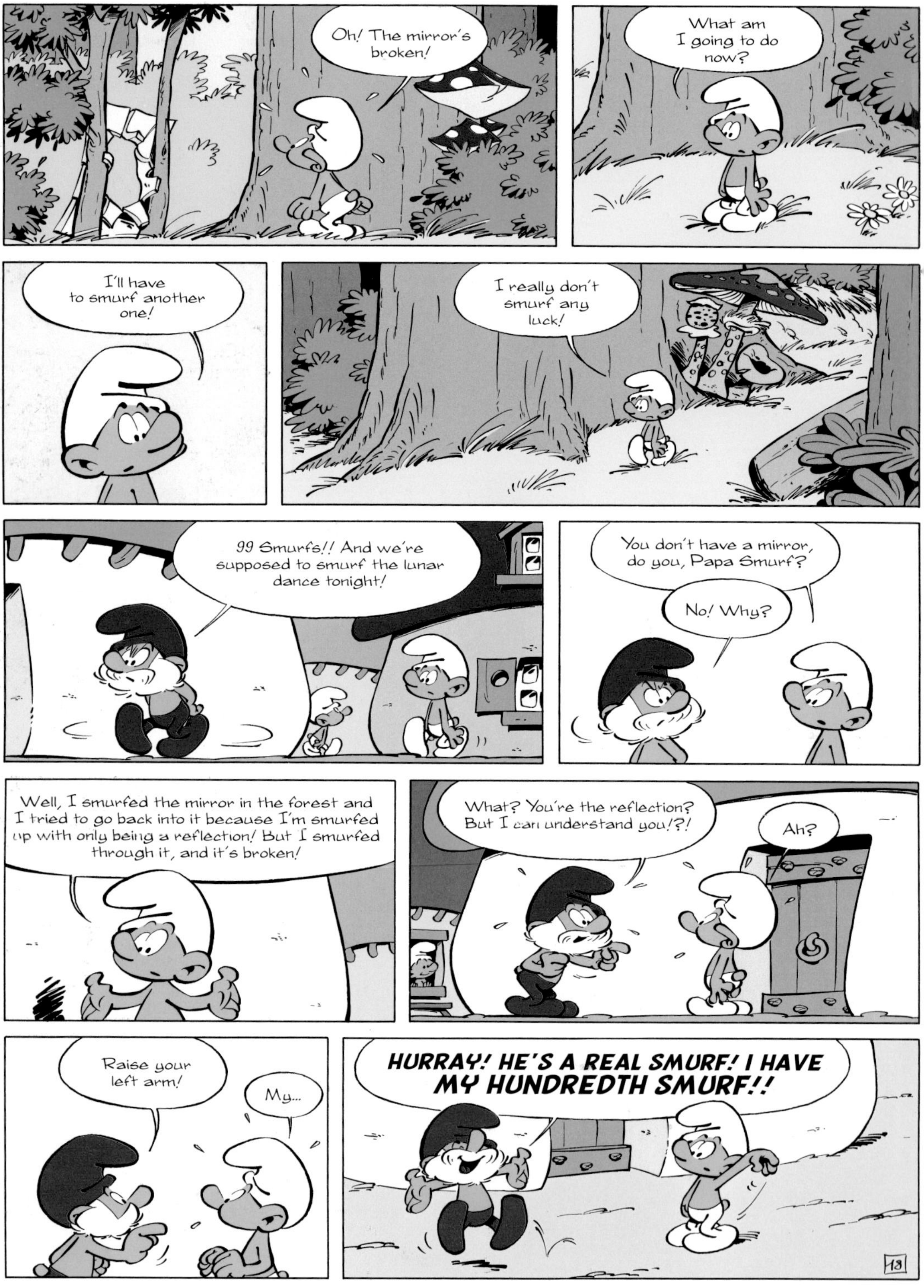
Oh! The mirror's broken!
What am I going to do now?
I'll have to smurf another one!
I really don't smurf any luck!
99 Smurfs!! And we're supposed to smurf the lunar dance tonight!
You don't have a mirror, do you, Papa Smurf?
No! Why?
Well, I smurfed the mirror in the forest and I tried to go back into it because I'm smurfed up with only being a reflection! But I smurfed through it, and it's broken!
What? You're the reflection? But I can understand you!?!
Ah?
Raise your left arm!
My...
HURRAY! HE'S A REAL SMURF! I HAVE MY HUNDREDTH SMURF!!
18

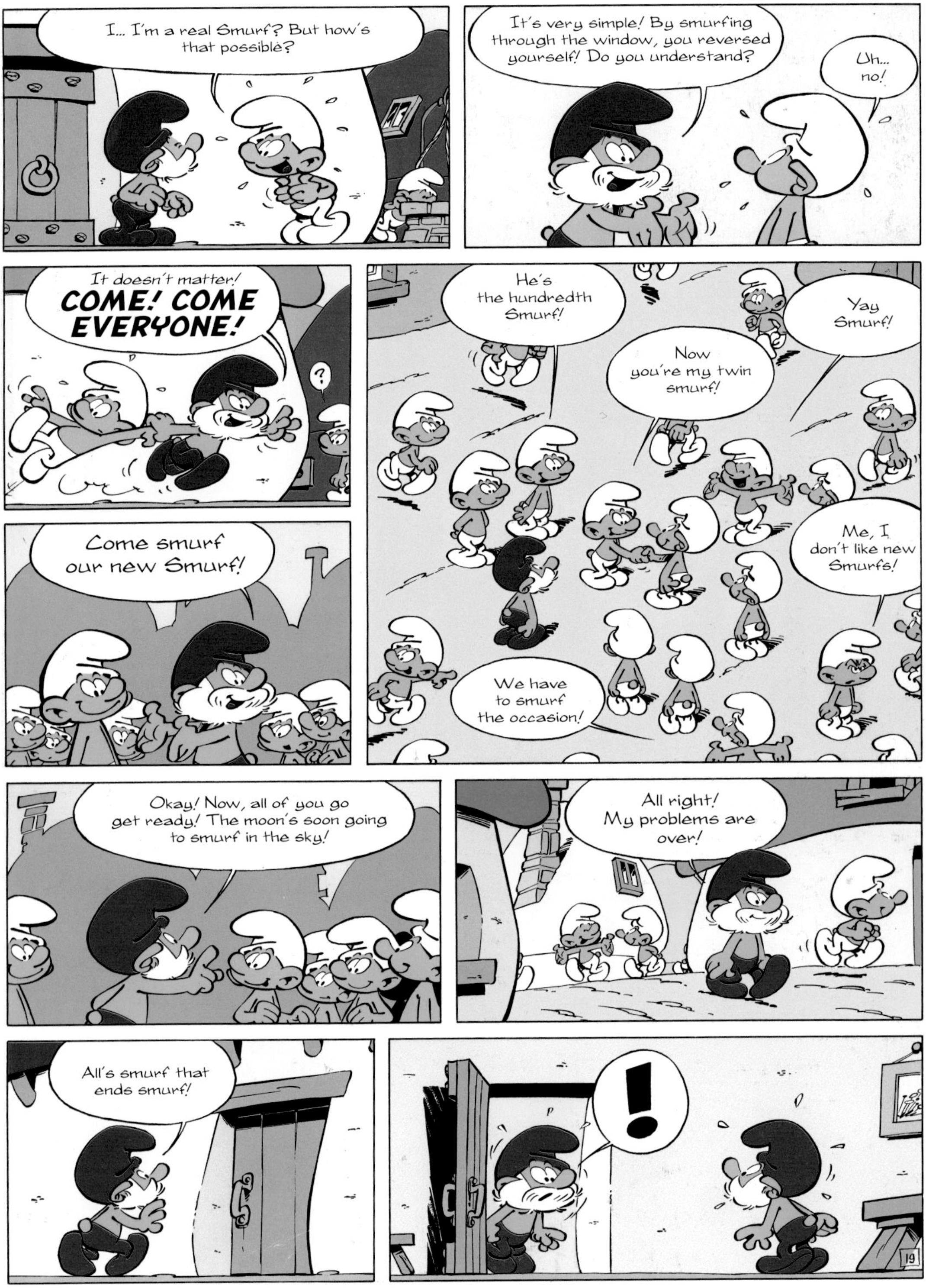
I... I'm a real Smurf? But how's that possible?
It's very simple! By smurfing through the window, you reversed yourself! Do you understand?
Uh... no!
It doesn't matter! COME! COME EVERYONE!
?
He's the hundredth Smurf!
Yay Smurf!
Now you're my twin smurf!
Me, I don't like new Smurfs!
We have to smurf the occasion!
Come smurf our new Smurf!
Okay! Now, all of you go get ready! The moon's soon going to smurf in the sky!
All right! My problems are over!
All's smurf that ends smurf!
!
19

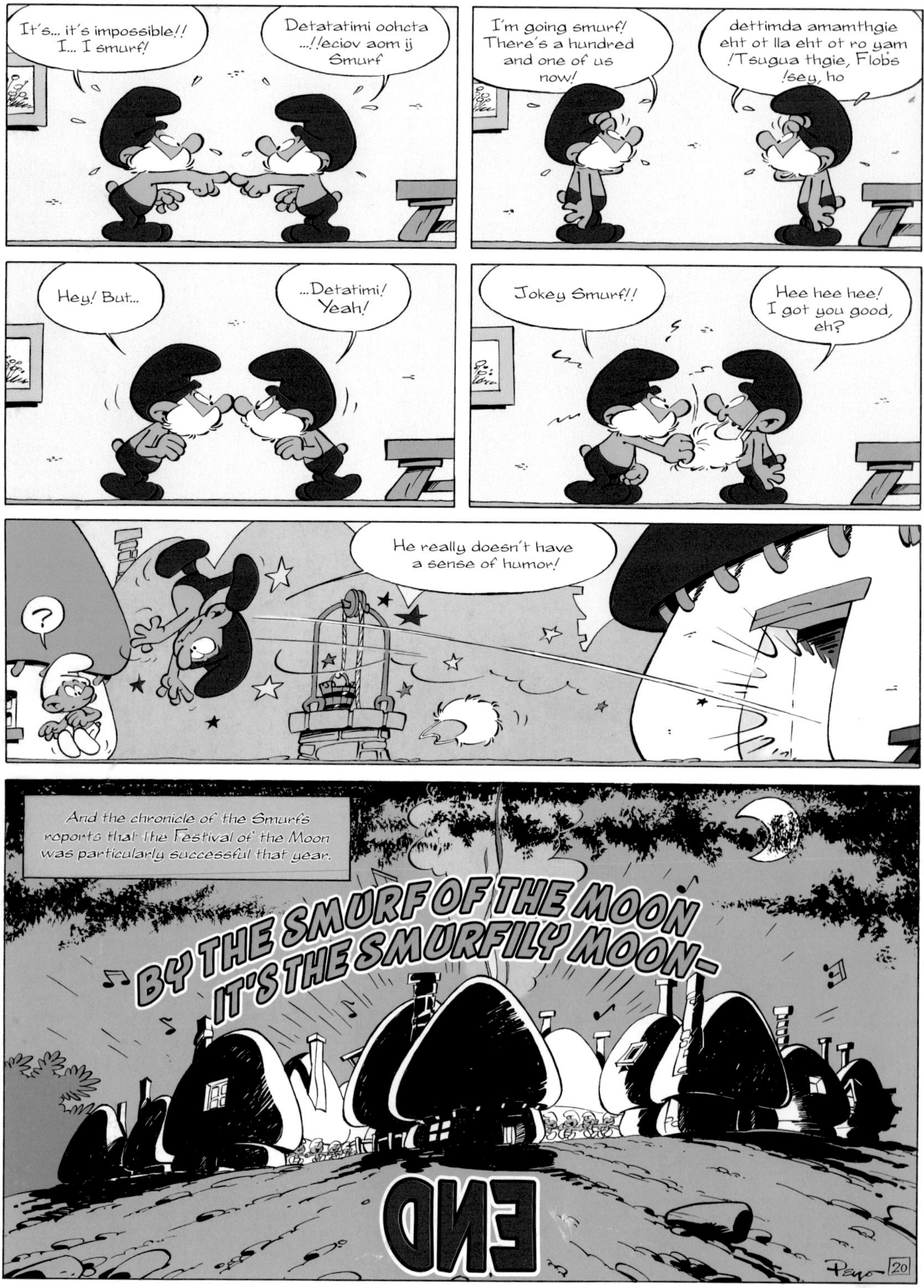
It's... it's impossible!!
I... I smurf!
Detatatimi oohcta
...!!eciov aom ij
Smurf
I'm going smurf!
There's a hundred
and one of us
now!
dettimda amamthgie
eht ot lla eht ot ro yam
!Tsugua thgie, Flobs
!sey, ho
Hey! But...
...Detatimi!
Yeah!
Jokey Smurf!!
Hee hee hee!
I got you good,
eh?
?
He really doesn't have
a sense of humor!
And the chronicle of the Smurfs
reports that the Festival of the Moon
was particularly successful that year.
BY THE SMURF OF THE MOON
IT'S THE SMURFILY MOON-
END
20